与自己和解
才能与世界温柔相处

【加拿大】斯蒂芬·里柯克 等 著
张白桦 译

洞见卷（中英双语）

世界微型小说精选

中国国际广播出版社

微型小说界的一个奇异存在

陈春水

张白桦，女，于 1963 年 4 月出生于辽宁沈阳一个世代书香的知识分子家庭，父亲是中国第一代俄语专业大学生。她曾先后就读于三所高校，具有双专业教育背景，所修专业分别为英国语言文学、比较文学与世界文学。她有两次跳级经历，一次是从初二到高三，另一次是从大一到大二。最后学历为上海外国语大学文学硕士，研究方向为译介学，师从谢天振教授（国际知名比较文学专家与翻译理论家、译介学创始人、中国翻译学创建人、比较文学终身奖获得者），为英美文学研究专家、翻译家胡允桓（与杨宪益、沙博理、赵萝蕤、李文俊、董乐山同获"中美文学交流奖"，诺贝尔文学奖得主托妮·莫里森世界范围内研究兼汉译第一人，翻译终身奖获得者）私淑弟子。她现为内蒙古工业大学外国语学院副教授、硕士研究生导师，并兼任中国比较文学学会翻译研究会理事、上海翻译家协会会员、内蒙古作家协会会员。张白桦于1987年开始文学创作，已在《读者》《中外期刊文萃》《青年博览》《小小说选刊》《青年参考》《文学故事报》等海内外一百多种报刊，以及生活·读书·新知三联书店、中译出版社、北京大学出版社、中国国际广播出版社，公开出版以微型小说翻译为主，包括长篇小说、中篇小说、散文、随笔、诗歌、杂文、评论翻译和原创等在内的编著译作36部，累计1200万字。

在中国微型小说界，众所周知的是：以性别而论，男性译作者多，女性译作者少；以工作内容而论，搞创作的多，搞研究的少；以文学样式而论，只创作微型小说的作者多，同时创作长篇小说、散文、诗歌、文学评论的作者少；以作者性质而论，搞原创的多，搞翻译的少；以翻译途径而论，外译汉的译者多，汉译外的译者少；以译者而论，搞翻译的人多，同时搞原创的人少。而具备上述所有"少"于一身的奇异存在，恐怕张白桦是绝无仅有的一位。

张白桦是当代中国微型小说第一代译作者，也是唯一因微型小说翻译而获奖的翻译家。其译作量大质优，覆盖面广泛，风格鲜明，具有女性文学史、微型小说史意义；是中国第一个从理论上，从宏观和微观层面，论证当代外国微型小说汉译的文学史意义的学者，具有翻译文学史意义；小说创作篇幅涉及长篇、中篇、短篇、微型小说，创作的文学样式覆盖小说、散文、诗歌、文学评论等主要文学样式；是既有微型小说译作，又有微型小说原创的全能型译作家，且译作与原创具有通约性；还是微型小说英汉双向翻译的译作者。她的微型小说翻译实践开创了中国微型小说双向翻译的两个"第一"："译趣坊"系列图书为中国首部微型小说译文集，在美国出版的《凌鼎年微型小说选集》为中国首部微型小说自选集英译本。

2002年，其微型小说译著《英汉经典阅读系列散文卷》曾获上海外国语大学研究生学术文化节科研成果奖；1998年，其微型小说译作《爱旅无涯》获《中国青年报·青年参考》最受读者喜爱的翻译文学作品；她本人曾在2001年当选小小说存档作家、2002年当选为当代微型小说百家；微型小说译作《仇家》当选为全国第四次微型小说续写大赛竞赛原作；2012年，其译作《海妖的诱惑》获以色列第32届世界诗人大会主席奖等文学奖项；"译趣坊"系列图书深受广大青年读者喜欢。

此外，她的论文《外国微型小说在中国的初期接受》入选复旦大学出版社的《润物有声——谢天振教授七十华诞纪念文集》，以及湖南大学出版社的张春的专著《中国小小说六十年》续表。译作《门把手》入选春风文艺出版社出版的《21世纪中国文学大系2002年翻译文学》。译作《生命倒计时》入选春风文艺出版社出版的谢天振、韩忠良的专著《21世纪中国文学大系2010年翻译文学》。

张白桦关于外国微型小说的论文具有前沿性和开拓意义。例如，《外国微型小说在中国的初期接受》是国内对于外国微型小说在中国接受的宏观梳理和微观分析。《当代外国微型小说汉译的文学史意义》证实了"微型小说翻译与微型小说原创具有同样建构民族、国别文学发展史的意义，即翻译文学应该，也只能是中国文学的一部分"。她指出，当代外国微型小说汉译的翻译文学意义在于："推动中国当代的主流文学重归文学性，重归传统诗学的'文以载道'的传统；引进并推动确立了一种新型的、活力四射的文学样式；当代微型小说汉译提高了文学的地位，直接催生并参与改写了中国当代文学史，以一种全新的文体重塑了当代主流诗学。"

其论文也反映出张白桦的文学翻译观和文学追求，例如，在《外国微型小说在中国的初期接受》中，她说："吾以吾手译吾心。以文化和文学的传播为翻译的目的，以妇女儿童和青年为目标读者，让国人了解世界上其他民族的妇女儿童和青年的生存状态。以'归化'为主，'异化'为辅的翻译策略，全译为主，节译和编译为辅，突出译作的影响作用和感化作用，从而形成了简洁隽永、抒情、幽默、时尚的翻译风格。与此同时，译作与母语原创的微型小说，在思想倾向、语言要素、风格类型和审美趣味上形成了通约性和文化张力，丰富了译作的艺术表现力和感染力。"

在《当代外国微型小说汉译的文学史意义》中，她说："文学翻译是创造性叛逆，创造性叛逆赋予原作以第二次生命。处于文学样式'真空状态'的中国第一代微型小说译者一方面充分发挥了翻译的主体性作用，挥洒着'创造性叛逆'所带来的'豪杰'范儿，对于原文和原语文化'傲娇'地'引进并抵抗着',有意和无意地遵循着自己的文学理想和审美趣味'舞蹈'着,为翻译文学披上了'中国红'的外衣,在内容和形式上赋予译作一种崭新的面貌和第二次生命。一方面在原文、意识形态、经济利益、诗学观念的'镣铐'上,'忠实'并'妥协'着。"

著名评论家张锦贻在《亭亭白桦秀译林》中说:"张白桦所译的作品范围极广,涉及世界各大洲,但选择的标准却极严,注重原作表现生活的力度和反映社会的深度。显然,张白桦对于所译原作的这种选择,绝不仅仅是出于爱好,而是反映出她的审美意识和情感倾向。她着力在译作中揭示不同地区、不同国度、不同社会、不同人种的生存境况和心理状态,揭示东西方之间的文化差异和分歧,都显示出她是从人性和人道的角度来观察现实的人生。而正是通过这样的观察,才使她能够真正地去接触各国文学中那些反映社会底层的大众作品,才能使她真正地关注儿童和青年,也才使她的译作真正地走向中国的民众。事实证明,译作的高品位必伴以译者识见的高明和高超。脱了思想内核,怕是做不好文学译介工作的。……类似的译作比比皆是,到后来,就是事先不知道译者,几行读下来,亦能将她给'认出来'。也就是说,张白桦在选择原作和自己的翻译文字上都在逐步形成一种独具的风格。……使她能够在不同的译作中巧用俚语,活用掌故,借用时俗。她善于用中国人最能领会的词语来表达各式各样的口吻,由此活现出不同人物的身份和此时此刻的心神和表情；她也长于用青少年最能领悟的词句来表达不同的侧面，同时展现出不同社会的氛围和当时当地的风习。"

胡晓在《中国教育报》发表的《学英语您捕捉到快乐了吗》中说："我最喜欢她的译作，因为所选篇目均为凝练精巧之作，难易适中，且多是与生活息息相关的内容，能够极大限度地接近读者。所选的文字皆为沙里淘金的名家经典，文华高远，辞采华丽。名家的经典带来的是审美的享受和精神的愉悦，含蓄隽永的语句令人不由得会心一笑；至真至纯的爱与情，轻轻拨动着人们的神经；睿智透彻的思考，让人旷达而超脱。"

综上所述，在微型小说的文化地理中，张白桦是一个独特的所在。她以独特的文化品相，承接了中华与西洋的博弈，以理论和实践造就的衍生地带，自绘版图却无人能袭。

（作者系中国作协会员，小小说作家网特约评论家，第六届小小说金麻雀提名奖获得者，本篇原载于中国作家网2015年9月9日。网址：http://www.chinawriter.com.cn）

没有微型小说汉译就没有当代微型小说

——张白桦访谈录

陈勇（中国作协会员，小小说作家网特约评论家，第六届小小说金麻雀提名奖获得者，以下简称陈）：我做微型小说评论多年，范围遍及世界华文微型小说界，您是我研究视野中出现的第一个微型小说翻译家，可能也是唯一的一个。

张白桦（以下简称张）：谢谢陈老师的青睐，我更加惊诧于您的学术识别力。因为，即使在外语界和翻译界，对于文学翻译的认识还是有许多误区的。难怪微型小说界的评论总是视译者为"局外人"，所以无人问津了。而从我的研究方向——译介学的角度来看，得出的结论是：微型小说翻译，特别是微型小说翻译文学，应该，也只是中国文学的一部分。

陈：我认同翻译与创作是国别文学的"鸟之两翼，车之两轮"之说。您能给大家普及一下文学翻译与文学创作的区别吗？

张：好的，我愿意。从文艺的本质规律来看，二者并没有分别。

从创作的内容来看，翻译的确比创作少了一道工序——构思。然而，也正是由于这一缺失，反而给翻译带来了创作所没有的困难。可以负责任地说，从创作的过程来看，正如许许多多20世纪三四十年代的作家兼翻译家共同体会到的那样，文学翻译比文学创作要难。

陈：我之所以选择了您作为评论对象，是由于您在微型小说界的独特地位和影响力，以及您在研究和实践层面全面开花的成果。

张：这倒是符合事实的。在实践方面，我在20世纪80年代初，也就是大三的时候，就翻译了第一篇微型小说，一直走下来，应该说与当代中国微型小说是共同成长的，又是唯一一个因此获奖的译者；此外，中国首部微型小说译文集"译趣坊"系列图书和中国首部微型小说自选集英译本《凌鼎年微型小说选集》也是我做的。在研究方面，是中国第一个从理论上，从宏观和微观层面，论证当代外国微型小说汉译的文学史意义的学人。

陈：您能把您的理论观点论述得详细些吗？

张：可以。当代外国微型小说汉译的翻译文学意义就在于：推动中国当代的主流文学重归文学性，重归传统诗学的"文以载道"的传统；引进并推动确立了一种新型的、活力四射的文学样式；当代微型小说汉译提高了文学的地位，直接催生并参与改写了中国当代文学史，以一种全新的文体重塑了当代主流诗学。

陈：哦，所以您才会下这样的判断："没有外国微型小说汉译，就没有当代微型小说。"是吗？

张：您的学术敏感度令人惊叹。

陈：根据我的调查统计分析，发现搞微型小说翻译实践的人虽然相对不多，却也还是有一些的。您能谈谈使您脱颖而出的"别裁之处"吗？

张：我是经历了实践—理论—再实践这样一个非线性的过程，它带给我的是对文学翻译本质的思考，对翻译艺术掌控力的把握，对文学翻译的全面观照。据我所知，微型小说译者的文化背景比较复杂，创作态度也良莠不齐。老一辈翻译家在语言文化基础和创作态度上是无可厚非的，基本表现为"全译"，可惜在文字上与原文"靠得太近"，人数也太少；中青年译者的数量居多，但语言文化基础大多不如前辈，在对原文的处理上"尺度过大"，多数表现为"编译"。

我生性保守，为人为文拘谨，记得曾经在《世界华文微型小说作家微自传》中这样总结过："回首往事，也算是'张三中'吧：'心中'的原文，'眼中'的译文，'意中'的师生。"换句话说，对原文的敬畏，对译文的时代化，对青年、妇女儿童读者的念念不忘，千方百计地贴近时代，可能因此造就我的译文忠实性和可读性较强，基本表现为"全译"。

陈：果然如此。在您的译作中，我发现有几个题材是您情有独钟的，比如，青年、妇女和儿童。也就是说，这是您自觉的文学追求，是您的"主观倾向"吧？

张：您一语中的。是的，身为女性，我"含泪的微笑"更多地落在了相似群体身上,是希望通过译作擦亮人文关怀的"镜与灯"。

陈:如果让您用几个关键词来概括您的翻译风格的话,您会选择哪些词?

张:首先进入我脑海的是:简洁、幽默、时尚。

陈:为什么是这三个词,而不是其他?

张:这个嘛,都源于我的"本色演出"。我这人简单直接,译文也就长不了;身为教书匠,我喜欢寓教于乐,译文也就搞文字狂欢;我的目标读者是青年,我的译文就各种"潮","一大波流行词语正在靠近"。

陈:嗯嗯,听出来啦。最后,我还是要不客气地指出您在创作趋势上的一个问题:您的微型小说翻译在初期量大质优,"凡有井水处,皆能歌柳词",而近期在数量上却大不如前了,希望您可以有所弥补。

张:谢谢陈老师指教,我也意识到了这个问题。原因是多方面的,最重要的还是我目前的长篇著译、教学和研究生辅导让我分身乏术。不过,我一定竭尽心力,在理论上继续为微型小说翻译"鼓与呼",在实践上做"颜色不一样的烟火"。

(本篇原载于中国作家网 2015 年 9 月 9 日。网址:http://www.chinawriter.com.cn)

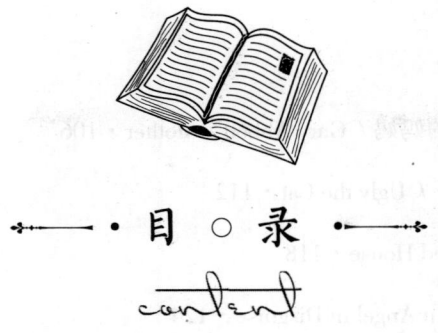

目 录
content

黄昏 / Dusk・1

一双丝袜 / A Pair of Silk Stockings・12

火车奇遇 / Your Inner Voice・20

痴迷旅行 / Why My Addiction to Travel Has Kept Me Single・25

99 元俱乐部 / The 99 Club・34

背景 / The Background・39

"独角兽" / The Unicorn・49

猫之禅 / The Zen of Cat・56

泄密的心 / The Tell-Tale Heart・61

希望与安慰 / Hope and Comfort・73

老鼠 / The Mouse・84

不舒服的床 / An Uncomfortable Bed・91

你准备好了吗 / Are You Ready・99

I

加里·阿伯特的妈妈 / Gary Abbott's Mother·106

流浪猫"丑丑" / Ugly the Cat·112

鬼屋 / A Haunted House·118

天使的伪装 / An Angel in Disguise·124

我的导师 / My Masters·133

石匠 / Antonio Canova·138

小矮马和驴 / The Pony and the Donkey·147

幸运的礼服 / The Blessed Dress·153

做风筝的人 / Kite Maker·160

业余爱好者 / An Amateur·167

一夜惊魂 / What a Night·173

命中注定的"爱" / "Love" Meant to Be…·180

怎样才能活到200岁 / How to Live to Be 200·187

田岛 / TAJIMA·196

最后一次送货 / The Last Delivery·208

永远不要杀害作者 / Never Kill the Author·213

译后记·223

黄 昏

[英国] 萨基

  诺尔曼·葛尔特茨比坐在海德公园的长凳上，前面宽阔的马路对面，是一家 The Row 品牌店。这是三月初的一个傍晚，大约六点半。暮色四合，只有那微弱的月光和点点星光冲淡着天色的昏暗。马路和人行道都空空荡荡的。然而，就在这若明若暗的夜色中仍有不少被人们遗忘的小人物在活动着。他们有的游来荡去，无声无息；有的点缀在长凳和木椅上，并不引人注目。在昏暗中，他们坐在那里的身影已经无法辨认清楚。

  眼前的景色让葛尔特茨比很满意，与他此刻的心情非常契合。在他看来，黄昏，是失败者的时刻。男男女女，奋斗过，失败过，在这日薄西山的时候纷纷出来活动。他们把失掉的好运、破灭的希望深深地掩藏起来，躲避着好奇者的寻根问底。他们寒酸的衣衫、塌下来的双肩、不开心的目光，在朦胧的暮色中不会引起人们的注意，他们至少不会被别人认出来。

  长凳另一端，就在他身旁，坐着一位老先生。从他的神态里，可以看出他与社会抗衡的劲头已经消退，残余的那点个人的自尊已经不足以与任何人或任何事抗衡了。坐了一会儿，老人起身离去。远去的背影慢慢消失在黑暗中。空出来的位子几乎立刻被一个年轻人占据了。年轻人衣着虽然比较考究，但是他面部的神情并不比那位老人开朗。新来的人一屁股坐在长凳上，同时还能听见他恶狠狠地骂了一声，好像是要强调：这个世界待他不公。

"你看来心情不大好啊。"葛尔特茨比说道，心里揣摩着年轻人作秀是为了引起他适度的注意。

年轻人转过身来，脸上的不设防、坦荡不会令人生疑。但是葛尔特茨比反而因此一下子警觉了起来。

"要是你陷入我的困境，心情也好不了，"他回答说，"我干了有生以来最傻的一件事。"

"什么事？"葛尔特茨比不动声色地问道。

"我今天下午刚到伦敦，本打算在伯克夏广场的伯塔刚尼安饭店住下来，"年轻人接着说，"可是到了那儿我才发现，饭店在几个星期前就给拆掉了，在原址上盖起了一家影剧院。出租车司机给我介绍了另一家距离更远的旅店，我去了。我刚给家里人写完了一封信，告诉他们我的地址，就出去买香皂了——我忘了带香皂，又不喜欢旅店里的香皂。我在街上随便走了走，在酒吧喝了杯酒，又逛了逛商店，然后转身回旅店。就在这时候忽然意识到，我根本没记住旅店叫什么，更不知道它坐落在哪条街上。我在伦敦无亲无故，这太尴尬了。当然了，我可以打电报给家里人，叫他们把地址告诉我。可是这封电报明天才能收到，而眼下我身上几乎没钱了，我出来的时候，身上只带了一先令。买了块香皂，喝了杯酒，也就花得差不多了，我口袋里只剩下两便士，晚上都没有住的地方了。"

年轻人讲完这段故事后，有意地停顿了一下。"你大概想，我在编故事，不可能有这样的事吧？"年轻人随后说道，口气里有怨恨的意味。

"这事也并非不可能,"葛尔特茨比像法官审理案件似的说,"记得有一次我在国外,在一个国家的首都也做了这么档子事儿。不过那次我们一行两人,事情显得更离奇了。幸好我们还记得旅店紧靠着一条什么运河。一找到运河,我们就能找到回旅店的路了。"

听完这段往事的叙述,年轻人精神为之一振。"要是在国外,我还不会这么发愁,"他说道,"总可以找到领事馆,从那里得到必要的帮助。可是在自己国家,一旦陷入困境,只能露宿街头,在河堤上过夜了。除非能找到个像样的人,他能相信确有其事,借给我点钱。不管怎么说,我很高兴,因为您并没有认为我的故事不正常、难以置信。"

年轻人往这最后一句话里倾注了不少热情,就好像他有意向葛尔特茨比表示,葛尔特茨比基本上已经具备了像样的人的必要条件。

"然而,"葛尔特茨比慢吞吞地说,"这段故事的破绽就在于您拿不出那块香皂来。"

年轻人连忙向前探身,忙不迭地在大衣口袋里摸了起来。最后他一下子跳了起来。"我一定是把它弄丢了。"他怒气冲冲地嘟囔了一声。

"一个下午就丢了家旅店,又丢了块香皂,这只能说明你是故意这么马大哈的。"葛尔特茨比说道,可是年轻人没等他话音落下就走了。他顺着小路溜掉了,头昂得高高的。不过,那神情里有自尊,有疲惫。

"真遗憾,"葛尔特茨比若有所思地自言自语,"整个故事中只有自己出去买香皂这一点有说服力,可也正是在这个细节上他露了马脚。他要是深谋远虑、有先见之明的话,就应该事先准备一块香皂,包装和封记等,所有的一切都要跟刚从柜台上买来的一样,那他准可以成为这个特殊行当里的天才人物。干他这个特殊的行当,自然是应该每个细节都考虑周全、有备无患。具备这种无穷的能力,就是天才。"

想到这里，葛尔特茨比站了起来，准备离去。就在这时，他禁不住喊了一声，语气里透出了一丝担忧。只见在长凳边的地上，有一个椭圆形的小纸包，外表上有商店主人精心打上的封记和包装以及一切。不是香皂，还能是什么？显而易见，是那个年轻人一屁股坐下来的时候从衣兜里掉出来的。葛尔特茨比一分钟都没耽搁，立刻顺着那暮色笼罩着的小路飞也似的追了过去，焦急地寻找着穿浅色大衣的年轻人的踪影。就在他遍寻不见，已经准备放弃时，忽然他发现要找的那个人正迟疑地站在马车道的路边上。显而易见，年轻人在犹豫，是从海德公园穿过去好呢，还是穿过耐茨布里支熙熙攘攘的人行道。听到葛尔特茨比招手喊他，他猛然转过身来，那神态里有敌意，也有自卫。

"能证明你故事真实性的重要证人出现了。"葛尔特茨比说道，伸出手来把香皂递了过去。"一定是你坐下来的时候从大衣口袋里掉出来的。是你走了以后，我在地上发现的。我曾经对你不信任，你一定要原谅我。那时一切证据都对你不利。如今，既然我听取了香皂的证词，我想我也应当服从它的判决。如果我借给你一枚20先令的金币对你能有点帮助的话……"

年轻人急忙接过金币，放进口袋，一切疑虑都排除了。

"这是我的名片，上面有我的地址，"葛尔特茨比继续说道，"你这星期哪天还钱都可以。这是你的那块香皂。可别再丢了，它可是你的好朋友啊。"

"幸好让你找着了。"年轻人说道。接着，几句感激不尽的话脱口而出，声音里有些古怪，随即他朝着耐茨布里支方向跑开了。

"可怜的孩子，差点儿哭出声来，"葛尔特茨比自言自语地说，"不过，这也不奇怪，困境中脱身，如释重负，安慰来得太突然。这对我也是个教训，不能自作聪明，不能仅仅凭当时的情况就给一个人下判断。"

葛尔特茨比顺着原路返回。经过戏剧性一幕的发生地——那条长凳时,他看到一位老先生在长凳下面看来看去,捅来捅去。葛尔特茨比认出这就是刚才同他坐在一起的那位老人。

"您丢什么东西了,先生?"他问道。

"是啊,先生,丢了一块香皂。"

Dusk

By SAKI

Norman Gortsby sat on a bench in the Park, with his back to a strip of bush-planted sward, fenced by the park railings, and the Row fronting him across a wide stretch of carriage drive. It was some thirty minutes past six on an early March evening, and dusk had fallen heavily over the scene, dusk mitigated by some faint moonlight and many street lamps. There was a wide emptiness over road and sidewalk, and yet there were many unconsidered figures moving silently through the half-light, or dotted unobtrusively on bench and chair, scarcely to be distinguished from the shadowed gloom in which they sat.

The scene pleased Gortsby and harmonised with his present mood. Dusk, to his mind, was the hour of the defeated. Men and women, who had fought and lost, who hid their fallen fortunes and dead hopes as far as possible from the scrutiny of the curious, came forth in this hour of gloaming, when their shabby clothes and bowed shoulders and unhappy eyes might pass unnoticed, or, at any rate, unrecognised.

On the bench by his side sat an elderly gentleman with a drooping air of defiance that was probably the remaining vestige of self-respect in an individual who had ceased to defy successfully anybody or anything. As he rose to go, retreating figure vanished slowly into the shadows, and his place on the bench was taken almost immediately by a young man, fairly well dressed but scarcely more cheerful of mien than his predecessor. As if to emphasise the fact that the world went badly with him the new-corner unburdened himself of an angry and very audible expletive as he flung himself into the seat.

"You don't seem in a very good temper," said Gortsby, judging that he was expected to take due notice of the demonstration.

The young man turned to him with a look of disarming frankness which put him instantly on his guard.

"You wouldn't be in a good temper if you were in the fix I'm in," he said, "I've done the silliest thing I've ever done in my life."

"Yes?" said Gortsby dispassionately.

"Came up this afternoon, meaning to stay at the Patagonian Hotel in Berkshire Square," continued the young man, "when I got there I found it had been pulled down some weeks ago and a cinema theatre run up on the site. The taxi driver recommended me to another hotel some way off and I went there. I just sent a letter to my people, giving them the address, and then I went out to buy some soap—I'd forgotten to pack any and I hate using hotel soap. Then I strolled about a bit, had a drink at a bar and looked at the shops, and when I came to turn my steps back to the hotel I suddenly realised that I didn't remember its name or even what street it was in. There's a nice predicament for a fellow who hasn't any friends or connections in London! Of course I can wire to my people for the address, but they won't have got my letter till tomorrow; meantime I'm without any money, came out with about a shilling on me, which went in buying the soap and getting the drink, and here I am, wandering about with two pence in my pocket and nowhere to go for the night."

There was an eloquent pause after the story had been told. "I suppose you think I've spun you rather an impossible yarn," said the young man presently, with a suggestion of resentment in his voice.

"Not at all impossible," said Gortsby judicially, "I remember doing exactly the same thing once in a foreign capital, and on that occasion there were two of us, which made it more remarkable. Luckily we remembered that the hotel was on a sort of canal, and when we struck the canal we were able to find our way back to the hotel."

The youth brightened at the reminiscence. "In a foreign city I wouldn't mind so much," he said, "one could go to one's Consul and get the requisite help from him. Here in one's own land one is far more derelict if one gets into a fix. Unless I can find some decent chap to swallow my story and lend me some money I seem likely to spend the night on the Embankment. I'm glad, anyhow, that you don't think the story outrageously improbable."

He threw a good deal of warmth into the last remark, as though perhaps to indicate his hope that Gortsby did not fall far short of the requisite decency.

"Of course," said Gortsby slowly, "the weak point of your story is that you can't produce the soap."

The young man sat forward hurriedly, felt rapidly in the pockets of his overcoat, and then jumped to his feet. "I must have lost it," he muttered angrily.

"To lose an hotel and a cake of soap on one afternoon suggests wilful carelessness," said Gortsby, but the young man scarcely waited to hear the end of the remark. He flitted away down the path, his head held high, with an air of somewhat jaded jauntiness.

"It was a pity," mused Gortsby, "the going out to get one's own soap was the one convincing touch in the whole story, and yet it was just that little detail that brought him to grief. If he had had the brilliant forethought to provide himself with a cake of soap, wrapped and sealed with all the solicitude of the chemist's counter, he would have been a genius in his particular line. In his particular line genius certainly consists of an infinite capacity for taking precautions."

With that reflection Gortsby rose to go; as he did so an exclamation of concern escaped him. Lying on the ground by the side of the bench was a small oval packet, wrapped and sealed with the solicitude of a chemist's counter. It could be nothing else but a cake of soap, and it had evidently fallen out of the youth's overcoat pocket when he flung himself down on the seat. In another moment Gortsby was scudding along the dusk-shrouded path in anxious quest for a youthful figure in a light overcoat. He had nearly given up the search when he caught sight of the object of his pursuit standing irresolutely on the border of the carriage drive, evidently uncertain whether to strike across the Park or make for the bustling pavements of Knightsbridge. He turned round sharply with an air of defensive hostility when he found Gortsby hailing him.

"The important witness to the genuineness of your story has turned up, " said Gortsby, holding out the cake of soap, "it must have slid out of your overcoat pocket when you sat down on the seat. I saw it on the ground after you left. You must excuse my disbelief, but appearances were really rather against you, and now, as I appealed to the testimony of the soap I think I ought to abide by its verdict. If the loan of a sovereign is any good to you—"

The young man hastily removed all doubt on the subject by pocketing the coin.

"Here is my card with my address," continued Gortsby, "any day this week will do for returning the money, and here is the soap—don't lose it again it's been a good friend to you."

"Lucky thing your finding it," said the youth, and then, with a catch in his voice, he blurted out a word or two of thanks and fled headlong in the direction of Knightsbridge.

"Poor boy, he as nearly as possible broke down," said Gortsby to himself. "I don't wonder either; the relief from his quandary must have been acute. It's a lesson to me not to be too clever in judging by circumstances."

As Gortsby retraced his steps past the seat where the little drama had taken place he saw an elderly gentleman poking and peering beneath it and on all sides of it, and recognised his earlier fellow occupant.

"Have you lost anything, sir?" he asked.

"Yes, sir, a cake of soap."

一双丝袜

[美国]凯特·肖邦

一天,又瘦又矮的萨默斯太太意外捡到15美元。这对她来说算是一大笔钱了。这些钱把萨默斯太太那破旧的钱包撑得鼓鼓的,她觉得自己仿佛成了一位重要人物——她已经有许多年未曾体会过这种滋味了。

她仔细斟酌怎么用这笔钱。这一两天来,她一直处于一种梦幻般的状态,来回踱步,思考着各种选择。她可不愿意仓促行事,以免做出一些让自己后悔的事情。

只要再加一两美元就能凑足她平时给女儿贾妮买鞋子的钱,还能保证这双鞋子一定比平常买的耐穿许多。她可以给儿子们买布缝制新衬衫。女儿麦格也该买件上衣了。剩下的钱足够买几双新袜子——每个孩子两双。让全家人生平第一次打扮一新,这想法令她兴奋得坐立不安。

萨默斯太太深知寻找降价商品有多划算。但是那天她疲惫不堪,还有点虚弱。她来到大型百货商店,停留在一个冷清的柜台前,一只手搭在柜台上。

她没有戴手套。她慢慢意识到自己的手摸到了一些触感很舒服的东西。她低下头,看到自己的手正放在一堆丝袜上面。站在柜台后面的年轻女售货员问她是否想看看这些丝袜。

她微微一笑,仿佛她要买的是钻石首饰,别人请她查看珠宝似的。可她的手没停,继续抚摸着这轻柔而昂贵的商品,此时她用双手举起袜子,欣赏丝线间淡淡的荧光。

萨默斯太太挑了一双黑色的丝袜,仔细检查。

"1 美元 98 美分。"她大声说,"嗯,我要买这双。"

她递给售货员一张 5 美元的纸币,等待找零,顺便把袜子装好放进包装盒。这盒子可真小!放进萨默斯太太那个旧购物袋里仿佛消失了一般。

萨默斯太太随后搭乘电梯来到上一楼层的女士休息区。在一个没有人的角落,她脱下棉袜子,换上新买的丝袜。

这似乎是她平生第一次因为厌倦了计较斟酌而停歇下来。她让自己受控于某种机械力量,这股力量让她做出这一系列举动,将她从日常责任中解放出来。

丝绸贴在皮肤上的感觉真好!她真想就这样回去躺在柔软的椅子上,尽情享受那种丰富多彩的感觉。她穿上鞋子,把旧袜子装进袋子。接着,她走到皮鞋部,坐下来等待试穿。

她试穿了一双新靴子。

她把裙子撩到身后,将双脚转到一边,头则转到另一边,低头看着这对闪闪发光、鞋头尖尖的靴子。她的脚和脚踝看起来非常可爱,她简直不敢相信它们是自己身体的一部分。

买完新靴子,她来到了手套部。萨默斯太太已经很久没有戴过大小合适的手套了。她以前买的手套全都是"便宜货",便宜得根本无法期待它们的尺码适合她的双手。

一位年轻的女售货员把一只柔软的皮手套戴在萨默斯太太的手上,然后拉平到手腕位置,利索地扣上纽扣。有那么一两秒,这两个女人都迷失了，静静叹着这只小小的、戴着手套的纤纤玉手。

穿过街道时，她轻轻地提起裙摆。她的新袜子、新靴子和新手套让她的外貌产生了神奇的效果。它们带给她一种满足感，她觉得自己也成了衣着考究的那类人。

她感觉肚子饿得咕咕叫。换作从前，她准会忽略掉进食的欲望，等到了家再吃。但是那股引导着她的力量是绝不允许她有这种想法的。

街道转角处有一家餐厅。她注意到里面的白色桌布和闪闪发亮的玻璃杯，服务员正为富人们提供服务。

走进餐厅时，她的外表并没有引起吃惊或关注，虽然她进来之前还有点担心。

她在一张小餐桌前坐了下来。一位服务员立刻过来为她点餐。等待上菜的时候，她将手套慢慢脱下，放在一旁。

这里的一切都让人心旷神怡。桌布比隔着玻璃窗看到的还要白，还要干净，水晶酒杯也格外晶莹剔透。许多淑女与绅士在跟她一样的小餐桌上享用午餐，并没有注意她。

餐厅里传来一首悦耳的曲子，一阵微风透过窗户吹了进来。她尝了一口菜，缓缓地啜饮着红酒。她的脚趾头在丝袜里转动着。价格昂贵，但物有所值。

她吃完了饭，把算好的餐费递给了侍应生，还在他的盘子里多放了一枚硬币。他像对待拥有皇室血统的公主般朝她鞠躬致谢。

一切都结束了，如梦如幻。萨默斯太太走了过去，等候电缆车。

上了车以后，一位目光如炬的男士坐在她对面。他很难完全理解她脸上的表情。事实上，他什么也看不出来——除非他是一名魔术师，才能感受到她那让人心碎的愿望，她多么希望电缆车永远不会靠站，就这样载着她向前开，直到永远。

A Pair of Silk Stockings

By Kate Chopin

Little Mrs. Sommers one day found herself the unexpected owner of fifteen dollars. It seemed to her a very large amount of money. The way it filled up her worn money holder gave her a feeling of importance that she had not enjoyed for years.

The question of investment was one she considered carefully. For a day or two she walked around in a dreamy state as she thought about her choices. She did not wish to act quickly and do anything she might regret.

A dollar or two could be added to the price she usually paid for her daughter Janie's shoes. This would guarantee they would last a great deal longer than usual. She would buy cloth for new shirts for the boys. Her daughter Mag should have another dress. And still there would be enough left for new stockings—two pairs per child. The idea of her little family looking fresh and new for once in their lives made her restless with excitement.

Mrs. Sommers knew the value of finding things for sale at

reduced prices. But that day she was tired and a little bit weak. When she arrived at the large department store, she sat in front of an empty counter. She rested her hand upon the counter.

She wore no gloves. She slowly grew aware that her hand had felt something very pleasant to touch. She looked down to see that her hand lay upon a pile of silk stockings. A young girl who stood behind the counter asked her if she wished to examine the silky leg coverings.

She smiled as if she had been asked to inspect diamond jewelry with the aim of purchasing it. But she went on feeling the soft, costly items. Now she used both hands, holding the stockings up to see the light shine through them.

Mrs. Sommers chose a black pair and looked at them closely.

"A dollar and ninety-eight cents," she said aloud. "Well, I will buy this pair."

She handed the girl a five dollar bill and waited for her change and the wrapped box with the stockings. What a very small box it was! It seemed lost in her worn, old shopping bag.

Mrs. Sommers then took the elevator which carried her to an upper floor into the ladies' rest area. In an empty corner, she replaced her cotton stockings for the new silk ones.

For the first time she seemed to be taking a rest from the tiring act of thought. She had let herself be controlled by some machine-like force that directed her actions and freed her of responsibility.

How good was the touch of the silk on her skin! She felt like lying back in the soft chair and enjoying the richness of it. She put her shoes back on and put her old stockings into her bag. Next, she went to the shoe department, sat down and waited to be fitted.

She tried on a pair of new boots.

She held back her skirts and turned her feet one way and her head another way as she looked down at the shiny, pointed boots. Her foot and ankle looked very lovely. She could not believe that they were a part of herself.

After buying the new boots, she went to the glove department. It was a long time since Mrs. Sommers had been fitted with gloves. When she had bought a pair they were always "bargains", so cheap that it would have been unreasonable to have expected them to be fitted to her hands.

A young shop girl drew a soft, leather glove over Mrs. Sommers' hand. She smoothed it down over the wrist and buttoned it neatly. Both women lost themselves for a second or two as they quietly praised the little gloved hand.

She lifted her skirts as she crossed the street. Her new stockings and boots and gloves had worked wonders for her appearance. They had given her a feeling of satisfaction, a sense of belonging to the well-dressed crowds.

She was very hungry. Another time she would have ignored the desire for food until reaching her own home. But the force that was guiding her would not permit her to act on such a thought.

There was a restaurant at the corner. She had noted the white table cloths, shining glasses and waiters serving wealthy people.

When she entered, her appearance created no surprise or concern, as she had half feared it might.

She seated herself at a small table. A waiter came at once to take her order. While waiting to be served she removed her gloves very slowly and set them beside her.

It was all very agreeable. The table cloths were even more clean and white than they had seemed through the window. And the crystal drinking glasses shined even more brightly. There were ladies and gentlemen, who did not notice her, lunching at the small tables like her own.

A pleasing piece of music could be heard, and a gentle wind was blowing through the window. She tasted a bite, and she slowly drank the wine. She moved her toes around in the silk stockings. The price of it all made no difference.

When she was finished, she counted the money out to the waiter and left an extra coin on his tray. He bowed to her as if she were a princess of royal blood.

It was like a dream ended. Mrs. Sommers went to wait for the cable car.

A man with sharp eyes sat opposite her. It was hard for him to fully understand what he saw in her expression. In truth, he saw nothing—unless he was a magician. Then he would sense her heartbreaking wish that the cable car would never stop anywhere, but go on and on with her forever.

火车奇遇

这一天的开始,与我过去15年的每一天也没什么两样——起床、煮咖啡、淋浴、穿好衣服,出门赶7:35准时出发的火车,8:30到达工作单位。在火车上,我总会选择一个远离人群的座位,这样我就可以安静地看看报纸了。

在工作中,我总会受到来自同事、供应商的大量询问,还有那些可怕的电话和会议的轮番轰炸,所以我最不想做的事就是有那么个陌生人坐在我旁边,与我闲聊点儿什么。

我不清楚为什么,但出于某种原因,今天我上了火车就发现车上不同寻常,竟坐满了乘客,我不记得以前是否出现过这种情况。我犹豫了一下,然后在一位中年男士旁唯一的空位上坐了下来。当时,这位中年男士正低着头,似乎陷入了沉思。我坐下时,他仍继续看着地板,我很高兴他没注意到我。

没多久,火车就沿着我去市区的方向行驶了30分钟,我发现自己开始好奇这个人正在想什么。有什么事如此重要,连我在他身边坐下他都没看到?我试图忘掉这个念头,就开始读报。然而,出于某种奇怪的原因,这种"内心的声音"一直在促使我和这个人交谈。我试着忽视这个"声音",因为我不知道该怎么与一个完全陌生的人搭讪。

正如你可能猜到的那样,我最后终于克服了心理障碍,找了一个借口，向他提出了一个问题。当他抬起头，眼睛转向我时，我可以看得出他一定是真的很伤心，他双眼红红的，泪水从脸颊滚落下来，尽管他还在徒劳地尝试着擦去泪水。当我看到有人这么痛苦时，我内心的悲伤难以名状。

我们聊了大约20分钟，最后他似乎心情好多了。我们下车时，他千恩万谢，感谢我能够花时间陪他说话，成为他的天使。我根本没有从交谈中发现他的心情如此沉重的原因，但还是很高兴自己那天听从了内心的那个"声音"。

几星期过去了，一天，我吃完午餐回到办公室，发现办公桌上放着一个信封。信封上没有收信人姓名，只写着"天使收"。我的接待员附上了一张纸条，大意是：一位先生留下了这封信，说他不知道我的名字，但把我的外形描述得非常细致，所以接待员猜出这封信是给我的。

当我读完信封里的纸条以后，内心思绪万千，久久不能平静。原来这封信来自我在火车上遇到的那个人，他在信中再次感谢了我那天能够与他交谈，挽救了他的生命。

显然，他遇到了一些让他肝肠寸断的个人问题，这些问题已经几乎把他压垮，他打算就在那天结束自己的生命。他在信中接着解释说，他是个信仰宗教的人，也曾绝望地向上帝呼喊，如果上帝真的关心他，就会派人来阻止他自杀。在他眼里，我就是那个上帝派来的天使。

我本人并不信奉宗教，也不知道那个促使我尝试与一位陌生人交谈的内心"声音"代表着什么，但是我知道那个声音就在那天让某个人的生活发生了改变。因此，下次当你体会到那种促使你与一位朋友、一位亲人、一位邻居，或者甚至一位完全陌生的人交谈，却找不到任何明显理由的感觉时，请想想我的故事。倾听自己内心的声音，你可能会改变某个人的人生。

Your Inner Voice

My day started just like all the other days for the past 15 years where I get up, make some coffee, shower, get dressed and leave for the train station at precisely 7:35 A.M. to arrive at work by 8:30. While on the train I would always choose a seat away from the crowd so I can read the newspaper in peace and quiet.

At work I am always being bombarded with questions from co-workers, suppliers, telephone calls and then those dreaded meetings so the last thing I need is some stranger to sit beside me and start small talk.

I don't know why but for some reason when I got on the train today it was unusually full, something I don't recall ever happening in the past. With hesitation I sat down in the only seat available beside a middle-aged man that had his head down and seemed to be lost in his thoughts. I was glad that he didn't notice when I sat next to him as he just continued to look down towards the floor.

Shortly after the train left for my 30-minute ride downtown I found myself wondering what this man was thinking about. What could be so important that he didn't even see me sit next to him? I tried to forget about it and started to read my paper. However, for some strange reason this "inner voice" kept prompting me to talk to this man. I tried to ignore the "voice" as there was no way I was starting a conversation with a complete stranger.

As you probably guessed I eventually broke down and came up with an excuse to ask him a question. When he raised his head and turned his eyes towards me I could see that he must have been really upset as he had red eyes and still had some tears rolling down the side of his face despite his feeble attempt to wipe them away. I can't describe the sadness I felt seeing someone in so much pain.

We talked for about 20 minutes and in the end he seemed to be doing better. As we were leaving the train he thanked me profusely for being an angel by taking the time to talk. I never did find out what was making his heart so heavy with pain but was glad I listened to the "voice" that day.

Several weeks had passed when I noticed an envelope on my desk after returning from lunch. It was not addressed to anyone and only had the word "Angel" written on it. My receptionist attached a note saying a gentleman dropped it off saying he did not know my name but had described me well enough that the receptionist knew it was for me.

When I read the note inside the envelope I was so filled with emotions that I couldn't contain myself. It was a letter from the man I met on the train thanking me again for talking to him and saving his life that day.

Apparently he had some very hurtful personal problems that were so overwhelming he was planning to take his life that day. In his letter he went on to explain that he was a religious person and in desperation screamed out to God that if God really cared about him he would send someone to prevent him from taking his life. In his eyes I was that someone, that Angel sent by God.

Not being a religious person myself I don't know what that "voice" was that made me take a chance and talk to a stranger but I do know that it made a difference in someone's life that day. So the next time you feel prompted for no apparent reason to talk to a friend, relative, neighbor or even a complete stranger please remember my story. You just may make a difference in someone's life when you listen to your inner voice.

痴迷旅行

[美国]安娜贝尔·芬威克·艾略特

中世纪公认的最卓有成果的探险家——摩洛哥学者伊本·白图泰在 1354 年写下了以下文字，今天读来仍然如此真实，至少对我来说，那感觉跟 600 年前毫无二致：

旅行：它在 1000 个陌生的地方令你有归家之感，然后使你在自己的故乡成为孑孓一身的陌生人。

我从没想过要成为一名浪迹天涯的独行者，事实上，我一直以为到今年 31 岁时我将成为一名已婚母亲，擅长挑选沙发和墙纸款式。

而结果却是，我如今 31 岁了，却还是单身，还和妈妈住在一起，从来没有买过沙发，更不用说选购墙纸了。我曾经选择一生中花五年去环游世界，如今却放弃了所有的愿景（我当时哪能意识到这一点）。

我在为纽约一家报社撰文期间爱上了旅行写作，这完全是出于偶然的。我当时在生活栏目办公室，主要任务是编辑网络热传的猫视频、不可取的饮食和伊万卡·川普的鞋品收藏。当有个机会可以去哥斯达黎加为旅游部门审查一处丛林胜地时，我欣然接受了。

这是我首次独自踏上海外航程。把这个住地小屋形容为"乡村特色"会显得更亲切。我的房间只需在巨大热浪中攀登94级阶梯就到了，里面没有空调，但我有幸拥有三只常驻蜘蛛做伴，三只都个头儿很大，我还有一个小小的飞行蟑螂军团定期来访，它们整个晚上的行军目的地都很接近我的脸。

但我与房东的狗很快成了忘种之交，我在附近发现了一个宁静的海滩，我每天可以在漫漫长路上来回散步，我也想出办法把自己密封在毯子下以避免蟑螂的夜间来访，我迅速爱上了旅行的种种美好。不是去度假，而是去旅行，这在一定的年龄段（大学间隔年后、生孩子前），是非常自然的。如果你是单身，基本上你得独自完成旅程，没有你的朋友参与了。

我倒是一点也不介意。相反，我搬回伦敦，加入了报社的旅行写作团队。我20多岁的大部分生涯是在路上、在空中或在海上度过的，这里几个月、那里几个月，也回家待在大本营（我母亲的家），但我大部分的生活方式是提着旅行箱，进行有关旅行的写作。

我登上一艘去南极洲的船，跃入寒冷的冰山点缀的海洋；在南非时近在咫尺之间观看几只大白鲨；驱车穿过奥卡万戈三角洲时惊叹于狮子的雄壮；花了一个星期与猴子生活在一起；也曾在塔斯马尼亚森林扎营；重温了莫桑比克的一个蜜月岛；体验了迪拜的种种奇异风格；也看到了瑞典拉普兰的北极光。

在我开始这无疑令人艳羡的体验世界之旅前（这期间我踏遍每一个大洲，着迷于每个旅程），我的朋友大多都风流云散，或者单身一人待在家乡，穿梭于各种情感与关系之间，尝试各种尺寸的新生事物，就像拼字游戏一样重新排列和定位自己。

几年后当我回到报社办公桌后，游戏结束了，董事会也成立了。

我的大多数同龄人都成双成对了，他们中的许多人现在对沙发和墙纸有了深刻理解。

我在家里待着更感孤独，我在脸书上滑过无数的订婚虐狗通告，定期而慵懒地略过约会APP的门户网站，比我在1000个陌生的地方待着和真正只有一个人时更感孤单，一如600年前伊本·白图泰所描绘的那样。

参加情侣晚宴派对（CDP）现在是人们常做的一件事，然而当时像《BJ单身日记》女主布里奇·特琼斯那样，作为唯一的单身狗出现在餐桌上是了无生趣的。连去拜访我现已订婚的最好的闺蜜（这是我十年来几乎每天都在谈论的人，她知晓我灵魂中每一个尘土飞扬的角落，而我也深谙她的一切）现在也需要提前一个月预约，这充分体现了她CDP日记的分量。

这不仅仅是奇怪，也令我感到深深地难过。在这位最好的闺蜜结婚后不久，我那位出色的前男友死于脑瘤，我最好的闺蜜在最后一刻取消了带我去参加他追悼会的计划，因为她"没时间"。在旅行中我看到过很多非同寻常的东西，但这对我来说确是难以置信的惊人。这也是压垮骆驼的最后一根稻草，我们打那以后就没有再说过话，我的社交生活也变得更加安静，以至悄无声息。

我也听说过一些人在国外生活过一段后回到家乡的故事。那些20多岁的岁月是我们从象牙塔里走出来拼搏打下社会根基时雕砌塑型的，那是一段给我们深远影响的塑型岁月。我想念那些日子，感到很难在似水流年之后重新加入社群。

所以我继续尽可能多地去旅行，几乎总是独自一人。一路上我结交过亲密朋友，也经历过浪漫甜蜜。我如今仍然和他们保持着联系，他们都散落于千里之外的各个国家，但我的确仍然继续成为乡土故园里的一个陌生人。

　　至于为什么我还是单身，当然，除了我离开这么久这一事实之外，还有很多其他可能的原因。我有一颗不安分的灵魂，我固执己见。我在看电影期间太絮叨。直到最近，我都不知道原来斜倚在自己的飞机座位上会被认为是粗鲁的行为。

　　不过，话说回来，如果要拿来讨论的话，我没有男朋友是因为所有的旅行让我错过搭上滚滚红尘之船，这一切值得吗？我真的回答不了。是否应该结束一个无子嗣、身无分文的老姑娘身份，这是个无声地困扰着我的问题。但是坐回到另一架飞机上的难以满足的快感显然是我愿意为之付出的代价。

　　下个周末，我要去挪威北部探访一个偏僻小岛上与世隔绝的渔夫小屋，显然我也不太可能在那里找到白马王子，而那张空床正是我所选择的休憩之地。

　　旅行不再是过去的模式。世界是个地球村。

　　你有时要脚踏实地。当你这样做的时候，你才知道可以在旅行时与待在家里同样是一晌贪欢。

Why My Addiction to Travel Has Kept Me Single

By Annabel Fenwick Elliott

Moroccan scholar Ibn Battuta, widely considered to be the most prolific explorer of the Middle Ages, wrote this in 1354, and it feels as true today—to me at least—as it did more than six centuries ago.

Travelling: it gives you a home in a thousand strange places, then leaves you a stranger in your own land.

It was never my plan to become a lone planet wanderer. In fact, I always imagined that by now, at the age of 31, I'd be a married mother who was good at picking sofas and choosing wallpaper.

As it transpires, I'm 31, single, live with my mother, and have never procured a sofa, let alone chosen wallpaper. I gave up all prospects of that (not that I realised it at the time) when I opted instead to travel the world for five years of my life.

I fell into travel writing quite by accident, while working

for a newspaper in New York. I was on the lifestyle desk, largely covering viral cat videos, inadvisable diets and Ivanka Trump's shoe collection. When the opportunity arose to review a jungle resort in Costa Rica for the travel department, I gladly took it.

It was to be the first overseas voyage I ever set off on alone. To describe this lodge as "rustic" would be kind. My room was accessible only by clambering a total of 94 steps in the feverish heat, and it had no air-conditioning but was blessed with three resident spiders, all gargantuan in size, and a small army of flying cockroaches who paid regular visits to the close proximity of my face throughout the night.

But I befriended the owner's dog, found a quiet beach close by, took long walks, worked out a way to hermetically seal myself beneath the blanket to avoid the roaches at night, and promptly fell in love with the prospect of travel. Not going on holiday, but travel, which at a certain age (post gap year, pre babies) must by its very nature, if you're single, largely be done without your friends.

Not that I minded in the slightest. On the contrary, I moved back to London to join the newspaper's travel team and spent the majority of my twenties on the road, in the air, or at sea—with months here and there back home at basecamp (my mother's house) but most of it living out of a suitcase, and writing about it.

I joined a ship to Antarctica and leapt into the freezing iceberg-dotted ocean; came within feet of several great white sharks in

South Africa; drove through the Okavango Delta marvelling at lions; spent a week living with monkeys; camped in the Tasmanian forest; reviewed a honeymoon island off Mozambique; experienced the oddities of Dubai; and saw the northern lights in Swedish Lapland.

Before I embarked on this undeniably enviable foray around the world—during which I ticked off every continent, enthralled at every turn—most of my friends at home were scattered and single, darting between relationships, trying things on for size, rearranging themselves like Scrabble pieces.

By the time I was back behind my desk several years later, the game was over and the board was set. The vast majority of my peers had coupled up, and a surprising number of them by now knew an awful lot about sofas and wallpaper.

I felt far lonelier at home, scrolling past endless engagement announcements on Facebook and periodically peering half-heartedly through the portal of dating apps, than I ever did when I'd been, as Ibn Battuta put it, in a thousand strange places and truly on my own.

Couples dinner parties (CDP) were now a thing, and no fun at all to attend being the only Bridget Jones at the table. Seeing my now-betrothed best friend—the one I'd spoken to almost every day for a decade, who knew every dusty corner of my soul, and I hers—now required booking a month in advance, such was the weight of her CDP diary.

This wasn't just strange, it was profoundly sad. Shortly after said-best-friend got married, my wonderful ex-boyfriend died of a brain tumour, and she cancelled at the last minute plans to take me to his memorial service because she "didn't have time". I'd seen a lot of extraordinary things on my travels by now but this, to me, was truly staggering. It was the straw that broke the camel's back, we haven't spoken since, and my social life became quieter still.

I've heard the same stories from people who've returned to their hometowns after a stint of living abroad. Those years, wedged in our twenties as we emerge from university to lay our roots, are incredibly formative. Miss them, and it's hard to rejoin the pack later down the line.

And so I continue to travel, as often as I possibly can, almost always alone. I've made dear friends and had romances along the way. I still speak to these people, all of them distributed in various countries thousands of miles apart, but I really do remain, for the most part, a stranger in my own land.

As for why I'm still single, there are, of course, a plethora of possible reasons aside from the fact that I've been away so much. I'm restless and stubborn. I talk too much during movies. And until very recently, I had no idea that it was considered rude to recline one's plane seat.

But say, for argument's sake, that I'm without a boyfriend because all those travels made me miss the proverbial boat. Was it worth it? I really couldn't say. Ending up a childless, penniless spinster is a prospect that quietly haunts me. But the insatiable thrill of getting back on another plane is apparently a price I'm willing to pay.

Next weekend, I'm bound for the northern reaches of Norway, to review an isolated fisherman's cabin on a tiny, remote island. Obviously, I'm unlikely to find Prince Charming there. And that empty bed is one I've chosen to lie in.

Travelling is not what it was. The world is a global village.

You have to come down to Earth sometimes and when you do, you realize that inside, you're just as happy staying at home.

99元俱乐部

[澳大利亚]尼克

从前有一位国王,他每天过着穷奢极欲的生活,却从未感到快乐与满足。

一天,国王碰到一个边工作边快乐地歌唱的仆人。国王被迷住了。为什么自己作为这块土地上的最高统治者感到不快、沮丧,而这个地位低下的仆人会这么欢乐呢?

于是,国王问仆人:"你为什么这么快乐啊?"

仆人回答说:"陛下,我只不过是一个仆人,但我和家人并不需要太多的东西——能有一个遮风挡雨的住处和填饱我们一家人肚子的热饭,就足够了。"

国王并不满意这样的回答。当天晚些时候,他去向他最信赖的顾问征求意见。听完国王的苦恼和那个仆人的故事后,顾问说:"陛下,我相信这个仆人还没有加入99元俱乐部。"

"99元俱乐部?那是做什么的?"国王问道。顾问回答:"陛下,要想真正了解99元俱乐部,就要将99枚金币放入一个袋子,再把这个装有金币的袋子放到那个仆人的家门口。"

仆人看到袋子后,把袋子拿回了家。当他打开袋子的时候,欣喜若狂地喊了出来……这么多金币！

他开始数金币。数了好几遍之后，他终于确信这些金币总共有99枚。此时，他非常纳闷："没在袋子里的那第100枚金币去哪儿啦？肯定不会有人在袋子里只放99枚金币的！"

他四处寻找，把附近都找遍了，但仍然不见那最后一枚金币的踪影。最后，他终于精疲力竭，决定从今以后要比以前更加努力地赚钱，凑够这第100枚金币，完成他的收藏。

从那一天起，仆人的生活发生了改变。他每天拼死拼活地工作，脾气变得非常暴躁，还经常责怪他的家人不帮助他赚到那第100枚金币。不仅如此，他工作时再也没有唱过歌。

看到这一巨变，国王感到很困惑。当他寻求顾问的帮助时，顾问说："陛下，仆人现已正式加入了99元俱乐部。"

顾问继续说道："99元俱乐部属于那些有足够多快乐却永远不知足的人，因为他们总是渴望并追求那份额外的满足感，并告诉自己：'当我得到想要的最后那件东西时，我才会过上幸福的生活。'"

我们可以过着快乐的日子，即使我们所拥有的并不多，但从我们得到更大、更好的东西的那一刻起，我们就会想要得到更多！我们因此失去了睡眠，失去了快乐，还伤害了我们身边的人；这一切都是我们为自己不断增长的需求和欲望付出的代价。以上就是加入99元俱乐部的真相。

The 99 Club

By Nick

Once upon a time, there lived a King who, despite his luxurious lifestyle, was neither happy nor content.

One day, the King came upon a servant who was singing happily while he worked. This fascinated the King. Why was he, the Supreme Ruler of the Land, unhappy and gloomy, while a lowly servant had so much joy?

The King asked the servant, "Why are you so happy?"

The man replied, "Your Majesty, I am nothing but a servant, but my family and I don't need too much—just a roof over our heads and warm food to fill our tummies."

The King was not satisfied with that reply. Later in the day, he sought the advice of his most trusted advisor. After hearing the King's woes and the servant's story, the advisor said, "Your Majesty, I believe that the servant has not been made part of the 99 Club."

"The 99 Club? And what exactly is that?" the King inquired.

The advisor replied, "Your Majesty, to truly know what the 99 Club is, place 99 Gold coins in a bag and leave it at this servant's doorstep."

When the servant saw the bag, he took it into his house. When he opened the bag, he let out a great shout of joy… So many gold coins!

He began to count them. After several counts, he was at last convinced that there were 99 coins. He wondered, "What could've happened to that last gold coin? Surely, no one would leave 99 coins!"

He looked everywhere he could, but that final coin was elusive. Finally, exhausted, he decided that he was going to have to work harder than ever to earn that gold coin and complete his collection.

From that day, the servant's life was changed. He was overworked, horribly grumpy, and castigated his family for not helping him make that 100th gold coin. He stopped singing while he worked.

Witnessing this drastic transformation, the King was puzzled. When he sought his advisor's help, the advisor said, "Your Majesty, the servant has now officially joined the 99 Club."

He continued, "The 99 Club is a name given to those people who have enough to be happy but are never content, because they're always yearning and striving for that extra 1, telling to themselves: 'Let me get that one final thing and then I will be happy for life.'"

We can be happy, even with very little in our lives, but the minute we're given something bigger and better, we want even more! We lose our sleep, our happiness, we hurt the people around us; all these as a price for our growing needs and desires. That's what joining the 99 Club is all about.

背 景

[英国] 萨基

"我听那个女的说艺术行话听得够够的。"克劳维斯对他的记者朋友说道。"她总爱把某些电影说成是犹如一种真菌般会'上身'作祟的东西。"

记者说:"这倒让我想起了亨利·德里斯的事儿。我和你说过吗?"

克劳维斯摇了摇头。

"亨利·德里斯是土生土长的卢森堡大公国人。长大成人后,他成了一位销售代表。他经常去外国参加商业活动。一次他在意大利北部的一个小镇逗留时,家里传来消息说,一份来自远房已故亲戚的遗产落到了他的名下。

"尽管亨利·德里斯谦虚地认为那并非一大笔遗产,却也促使他把目光投向一些看似无害的奢侈品。这笔遗产尤其使他对当地艺术产生了浓厚的兴趣,安德里亚斯·宾西尼先生的文身针就是一个代表。宾西尼先生也许是意大利有史以来最杰出的文身工艺大师,但他的生活显然是一贫如洗。即便客户出价600法郎,他也会欣然设法满足客户的要求,从锁骨文到腰线,整个设计都充分体现了《伊卡洛斯的坠落》的耀眼风格。德里斯先生对最后完成的设计有点失望。他早就怀疑华伦斯坦在三十年战争期间攻克伊卡洛斯要塞，但是令他更满意的是宾西尼作品体现出的精湛技巧，这个作品被所有有幸目睹的人赞誉为宾西尼的杰作。

"那是他付出最大的努力，也是最后的努力所取得的成果。这位杰出的匠人甚至没等到拿到工钱就离开了人世，被埋在了一块装饰华丽的墓碑下。他那些带着翅膀的小天使没有为他最热爱的艺术留下一点发展空间。不过，那600法郎却是宾西尼的遗孀应得的。然而，销售代表亨利·德里斯的生活出现了重大危机。在无数小数目的催款要求下，那笔遗产已经少到不能再少。在还清一笔紧迫的酒钱和各种其他往来账款后，留给这位遗孀的只有430多法郎。这位夫人理所当然感到义愤填膺，正如她喋喋不休地解释的那样，不仅是由于被建议勾销的170法郎，还因为他想让她已故丈夫那件公认的杰作降价。过了一星期，德里斯不得不将他的开价降至405法郎，这让寡妇感到愤慨，不禁怒火中烧。寡妇取消了这次艺术品的交易，几天后，把这幅画赠给了贝加莫市政府。政府不胜感激地接受了。德里斯得知此事后十分震惊。他尽可能不引人注意地离开了城镇，到罗马出差时他才真正松了一口气。他希望他的身份和那幅名画在罗马都能被遗忘。

"但是他背负着那位已故天才给他的重任。一天，他出现在一家汗蒸房热气腾腾的走廊里，老板让他赶紧穿上衣服。这个老板是意大利北部人，他断然拒绝让名画《伊卡洛斯的坠落》在未经贝加莫政府允许的情况下公之于众。随着这件事被越来越多的人所知，公众对此的兴趣更浓了，政府官员也提高了警惕。在烈日炎炎、天气最热的下午，德里斯都不能到海里或河里游一小会儿泳，除非他穿上一件到锁骨的厚重泳衣。后来，贝加莫当局认为海水可能会损坏这幅杰作，于是颁布了一项永久禁令，禁止这位饱受骚扰的销售代表在任何情况下进行海水浴。总之,当他公司的老板们给他在波尔多附近找了一系列新的活动时,他感激涕零。然而,他的感激之情在法意边境戛然而止。一大批威风凛凛的官员禁止他离开,这让他想起一项禁止出口意大利艺术品的严厉法律。

"随后,卢森堡政府和意大利政府展开了一场外交谈判,欧洲局势因此乌云密布。但意大利政府立场坚定:它一点也不关心自身的命运,甚至不顾亨利·德里斯的死活,而坚决认为,《伊卡洛斯的坠落》(由已故的安德里亚斯·宾西尼创作)目前是贝加莫市的财产,不应离开该国。

"德里斯激动的情绪逐渐平复下来,但不幸的是,生性孤僻的他几个月后发现自己再次成为一场激烈争论的中心人物。一位德国艺术专家在贝加莫市获得了鉴定这幅著名杰作的许可,他声称这幅画是模仿宾西尼风格伪造的作品,可能是他晚年时期雇用的某个学生的作品。德里斯提供的这方面证据显然毫无价值,因为在长期的设计过程中他一直饱受传统麻醉剂带来的折磨。一家意大利艺术杂志的编辑驳斥了这位德国专家的观点,并且承诺证明他的私生活不符合任何体面的现代标准。整个意大利和德国都卷入了这场争端,欧洲其他国家很快也卷入了这场争论。西班牙议会会议上出现了激烈的争吵场面,哥本哈根大学授予这位德国专家一枚金牌(随后派出一个调查团对他的证据进行现场审查),而巴黎的两名波兰学生借自杀来表明他们对此事的看法。

"与此同时,这个人不幸的生活背景并没有比以前好多少,因此他沦落到意大利无政府主义者的行列中也就不足为奇了。他至少四次以一个危险且不受欢迎的外国人的身份被护送到边境,但他总是因《伊卡洛斯的坠落》(被认为是由安德里亚斯·宾西尼于 20 世纪初创作)被带回。然后有一天,在热那亚召开的无政府主义者大会上,一位同事在激烈的辩论中打破了一个装满腐蚀性液体的小瓶子倒在了他的背上。他穿的红色衬衫减轻了灼伤程度，伊卡洛斯却被毁得面目全非。攻击他的人因袭击一名无政府主义者同伴而受到严厉谴责，并因损毁一件国家艺术珍品而被判处七年监禁。亨利·德里斯一离开医院，就以一个不受欢迎的外国人的身份被送过了边境。

"在巴黎比较安静的街道上，尤其是美术部附近的街道，你有时会遇到一个神情沮丧、看起来忧心忡忡的人，如果你白天碰到他的话，他会带一点卢森堡口音回应你。他有幻觉，认为自己是《米洛的维纳斯》雕塑失去的一只断臂，希望能够说服法国政府买下他。在所有其他问题上，我相信他都是相当理智的。"

The Background

By SAKI

"That woman's art-jargon tires me," said Clovis to his journalist friend. "She's so fond of talking of certain pictures as 'growing on one', as though they were a sort of fungus."

"That reminds me," said the journalist, "of the story of Henri Deplis. Have I ever told it you?"

Clovis shook his head.

"Henri Deplis was by birth a native of the Grand Duchy of Luxemburg. On maturer reflection he became a commercial traveller. His business activities frequently took him beyond the limits of the Grand Duchy, and he was stopping in a small town of Northern Italy when news reached him from home that a legacy from a distant and deceased relative had fallen to his share.

"It was not a large legacy, even from the modest standpoint of Henri Deplis, but it impelled him towards some seemingly harmless extravagances. In particular it led him to patronize local art as represented by the tattoo-needles of Signor Andreas Pincini.

Signor Pincini was, perhaps, the most brilliant master of tattoo craft that Italy had ever known, but his circumstances were decidedly impoverished, and for the sum of six hundred francs he gladly undertook to cover his client's back, from the collar-bone down to the waist-line, with a glowing representation of the Fall of Icarus. The design, when finally developed, was a slight disappointment to Monsieur Deplis, who had suspected Icarus of being a fortress taken by Wallenstein in the Thirty Years' War, but he was more than satisfied with the execution of the work, which was acclaimed by all who had the privilege of seeing it as Pincini's masterpiece.

"It was his greatest effort, and his last. Without even waiting to be paid, the illustrious craftsman departed this life, and was buried under an ornate tombstone, whose winged cherubs would have afforded singularly little scope for the exercise of his favourite art. There remained, however, the widow Pincini, to whom the six hundred francs were due. And thereupon arose the great crisis in the life of Henri Deplis, traveller of commerce. The legacy, under the stress of numerous little calls on its substance, had dwindled to very insignificant proportions, and when a pressing wine bill and sundry other current accounts had been paid, there remained little more than 430 francs to offer to the widow. The lady was properly indignant, not wholly, as she volubly explained, on account of the suggested writing-off of 170 francs, but also at the attempt to depreciate the value of her late husband's acknowledged masterpiece. In a week's time Deplis was obliged to reduce his offer to 405 francs, which circumstance fanned the widow's indignation into a fury. She cancelled the sale of the work of art, and a few days later Deplis learned with a sense of consternation that she had presented it to the municipality of Bergamo, which had gratefully accepted it. He left the neighbourhood as unobtrusively as possible, and was genuinely relieved when his business commands took him to Rome, where he hoped his identity and that of the famous picture might be lost sight of.

"But he bore on his back the burden of the dead man's genius. On presenting himself one day in the steaming corridor of a vapour bath, he was at once hustled back into his clothes by the proprietor, who was a North Italian, and who emphatically refused to allow the celebrated Fall of Icarus to be publicly on view without the permission of the municipality of Bergamo. Public interest and official vigilance increased as the matter became more widely known, and Deplis was unable to take a simple dip in the sea or river on the hottest afternoon unless clothed up to the collarbone in a substantial bathing garment. Later on the authorities of Bergamo conceived the idea that salt water might be injurious to the masterpiece, and a perpetual injunction was obtained which debarred the muchly harassed commercial traveller from sea bathing under any circumstances. Altogether, he was fervently thankful when his firm of employers found him a new range of activities in the neighbourhood of Bordeaux. His thankfulness, however, ceased abruptly at the Franco-Italian frontier. An imposing array of official force barred his departure, and he was sternly reminded of the stringent law which forbids the exportation of Italian works of art.

"A diplomatic parley ensued between the Luxemburgian and Italian Governments, and at one time the European situation became overcast with the possibilities of trouble. But the Italian Government stood firm; it declined to concern itself in the least with the fortunes or even the existence of Henri Deplis, commercial traveller, but was immovable in its decision that the Fall of Icarus (by the late Pincini, Andreas) at present the property of the municipality of Bergamo, should not leave the country.

"The excitement died down in time, but the unfortunate Deplis, who was of a constitutionally retiring disposition, found himself a few months later once more the storm-centre of a furious controversy. A certain German art expert, who had obtained from the municipality of Bergamo permission to inspect the famous masterpiece, declared it to be a spurious Pincini, probably the work of some pupil whom he had employed in his declining years. The evidence of Deplis on the subject was obviously worthless, as he had been under the influence of the customary narcotics during the long process of pricking in the design. The editor of an Italian art journal refuted the contentions of the German expert and undertook to prove that his private life did not conform to any modern standard of decency. The whole of Italy and Germany were drawn into the dispute, and the rest of Europe was soon involved in the quarrel. There were stormy scenes in the Spanish Parliament, and the University of Copenhagen bestowed a gold medal on the German expert (afterwards sending a commission to examine his proofs on the spot), while two Polish schoolboys in Paris committed suicide to show what they thought of the matter.

"Meanwhile, the unhappy human background fared no better than before, and it was not surprising that he drifted into the ranks of Italian anarchists. Four times at least he was escorted to the frontier as a dangerous and undesirable foreigner, but he was always brought back as the Fall of Icarus (attributed to Pincini, Andreas, early Twentieth Century). And then one day, at an anarchist congress at Genoa, a fellow-worker, in the heat of debate, broke a phial full of corrosive liquid over his back. The red shirt that he was wearing mitigated the effects, but the Icarus was ruined beyond recognition. His assailant was severely reprimanded for assaulting a fellow-anarchist and received seven years imprisonment for defacing a national art treasure. As soon as he was able to leave the hospital Henri Deplis was put across the frontier as an undesirable alien.

"In the quieter streets of Paris, especially in the neighbourhood of the Ministry of Fine Arts, you may sometimes meet a depressed, anxious-looking man, who, if you pass him the time of day, will answer you with a slight Luxemburgian accent. He nurses the illusion that he is one of the lost arms of the Venus de Milo, and hopes that the French Government may be persuaded to buy him. On all other subjects I believe he is tolerably sane."

"独角兽"[①]

[英国]史蒂夫·洛克利

"独角兽"隐身在赫兰达的后街里,避开了那些常见的、窥探的目光,吸引着那些其他客栈不肯招待的酒徒:小偷和杀人犯,乞丐和流浪汉。然而,老板彼得·加林却很少遇到什么麻烦,他是外地人,多年前买下了这家经营不善的旅馆。他是个大块头,比六英尺还高,胸像酒桶一样,曾经的金发如今变成了灰白色。但"独角兽"从来没有遇到过什么麻烦倒不是因为他。所有在这里喝酒的人都知道,无论是"黑奶牛"旅馆或"允许携带武器"旅馆,还是分散在城市其他的旅馆,永远都不会允许他们进入,只要一出现失控的蛛丝马迹,肇事者就会被其他酒客驱逐。尽管加林看起来很凶,他却很讨厌暴力,目前这种形势对加林非常有利。

人们到赫兰达来的原因有很多:一些人希望为自己或家人创造更好的生活,另一些人则希望摆脱过去。加林属于第二类,虽然他已经摆脱了以前的生活,但他却无法忘记。一天深夜,来了一个身披厚重斗篷的陌生人,威胁他说如果他不采取任何行动,事情就会发生转变。

最后一位常客离开时,这位陌生人还坐在火炉旁。加林拿起那人

---

① 这是一个赫兰达的故事(A tale of Hranda),"独角兽"是一个旅馆的名字。

的空啤酒杯倒满啤酒，等着他起身。那人却没有离开的意思，加林感到心跳加快，害怕接下来会发生冲突。

"好久不见了。"那人说。

"不好意思？"加林说，竭力装出不认识这个人的样子，虽然他知道这绝对装不住。

"彼得·加林。"那人哈哈大笑，"我还以为你起码会把名字改了呢。"

"你一定说的是另一个同名的人。"彼得·加林答道，避免与他的目光对视。

"我不这么认为。"穿斗篷的人说，"在卡尔斯格勒，能瞒过刽子手的人并不多。"

除了对一切矢口否认之外，他也说不出什么，但矢口否认也无济于事。他认出那个人就是亚历克斯·特尔戈夫，同样，那个人也认出了他。"你想干什么？"

"一定要守口如瓶。"

"已经这么做了。"

"我不知道是否能相信你。"特尔戈夫说着，从腰带上拔出刀子站了起来。"你以为躲在这样一个地方就能逃之夭夭、一劳永逸了吗？"

加林后退了几步，害怕自己的死期已到，就在这时，后面传来沉重的靴子声，更增加了紧张气氛。两个高大的身影从吧台后面冲了出来，把两个杯子摔在石板地上撞得粉碎，陶器碎片散落在房间的另一头。椅子被打散了，桌子被掀翻了，不一会儿的工夫，亚历克斯·特尔戈夫就躺在了地板上，他的刀深深地插进了自己的胸膛。

特尔戈夫重重地倒在最近的椅子边，加林的两个救星把桌子摆正，把破碎的家具收拾起来。

"对不起。"其中一名男子说,他更担心的是造成的破坏,而不是现在躺在旅店地板上的那具尸体。

"看来我们担心你的安全是对的,"其中一名男子说,"当我们看见这位披斗篷的朋友没有马上出来时,我们决定绕到后面看看你是否安然无恙。"

"谢谢你。"加林说,但觉得言不尽意。

另一名男子跪了下来,扯下男人脸上的兜帽,露出他脖子上那根难看的绳状的烧伤疤痕。这是唯一骗过了刽子手的人,而刽子手是唯一能指认他的人。

"我以前从来没有见过他。"加林说,他知道自己终于可以开始忘记过去了。

The Unicorn

By Steve Lockley

The Unicorn was tucked away in the back streets of Hranda, out of sight of casual prying eyes and attracted the drinkers that other inns would not entertain: thieves and cut throats, beggars and vagabonds. And yet there was rarely any trouble for the landlord Piotr Garim, an incomer who had bought the run down business many years before. He was a big man, well over six feet tall and barrel chested, his once blond hair now running to grey. But it was not due to him that there was never any trouble in The Unicorn. All the men who drank there knew that they would never be allowed into The Black Cow or The Welcome Arms or any of the other inns scattered around the city and at the first sign of anything getting out of hand, the trouble makers would be ejected by their fellow drinkers. It was a situation that suited Garim well as despite his own appearance he detested violence.

People came to Hranda for many reasons; some were looking to make a better life for themselves or their families, others to get away from their past. Garim fell into the second category and although he had left his former life behind he could not forget it. The arrival of a heavy cloaked stranger late in the evening threatened to change matters if he did not take any action.

The stranger was still sitting beside the fire when the last of the regular customers left. Garim took the man's empty beer mug to add it the rest and waiting for him to rise. The man showed no inclination to move though and Garim felt his heartbeat increase, fearing the confrontation that he knew would follow.

"It's been quite a while," said the man.

"Sorry?" Garim said, trying to act as if he had no idea of who the man was, though he knew that the act was destined to fail.

"Piotr Garim," the man laughed. "I thought you would at least have changed your name."

"You must have the wrong Piotr Garim," Garim replied. Avoiding eye contact.

"I don't think so," the man in the cloak said. "There are not many men who cheat the hangman in Karlsgrad."

There was nothing he could say other than try to deny it all, but that would be useless. He recognised the man as Alex Turgov just as well as the man identified him. "What do you want?"

"To be sure that the secret is kept buried."

"It is already."

"I'm not sure that I can believe that," Turgov said, pulling the knife from his belt and rising to his feet. "Did you think that you would be able to escape forever by hiding away in a place like this?"

Garim backed away, fearing that perhaps his time had come when a commotion grew behind heralded by the sound of heavy boots. Two large figures rushed from behind the bar sending two mugs crashing to the flagstone floor, shattering on impact and firing shards of pottery across the room. A chair was broken a table overturned but in moments Alex Turgov was lying on the floor with his knife sunk deep into his own chest.

Turgov slumped into the nearest chair as his two saviour righted the table and gathered the remains of splintered furniture.

"Sorry," one of the men said, more concerned about the damage done than the fact that there was now a corpse on the inn floor.

"Looks like we were right to be a little concerned for your welfare," one of the men said. "When our friend in the cloak didn't come out straight away we decided to go around the back and make sure you were alright."

"Thank you," Garim said, feeling the words were inadequate.

The other man knelt down and pulled the hood from the man's face to reveal the ugly rope burn scar around his neck. The only man to cheat the hangman, and the hangman the only one left to identify him.

"Never seen him before," said Garim and he knew that at last he could start to forget.

猫之禅

[美国] 吉姆·韦利斯

男人非常伤心。他知道猫余下的日子屈指可数了。医生说已经无可救药,他应该把猫带回家,并尽可能地让他在剩下的时间里过得舒服些。

男人摩挲着腿上的猫,幽幽长叹。猫睁开眼睛,呼噜呼噜地叫着,仰望着男人。一滴眼泪从男人的脸颊边滑下,落在了猫的额头上。猫有点不快地看了他一眼。

"你为什么哭呀,伙计?"猫问道。"因为你一想到即将失去我就难以承受?因为你认为你永远都不能找到可以代替我的猫?"男人点了点头,"是的。"

"那么你认为我离开你以后,会到什么地方去呢?"猫问道。男人无助地耸了耸肩。"闭上眼睛吧,伙计。"猫说。男人用探询的目光看了他一眼,不过还是顺从地闭上了眼睛。

"我的眼睛和毛皮是什么颜色的啊?"猫问。"你的眼睛是金色的,你的毛皮是浓郁而温暖的褐色。"男人回答道。

"那你最常在什么地方见到我呢?"猫问。"我经常见到你……在厨房的窗台上看鸟……在我最喜欢的椅子上……躺在桌子上我需要用的文件上……晚上睡在我脑袋边的枕头上。""那么,以后无论什么时候你想见我,只要闭上你的眼睛就可以了。"猫说道。

"把地上的那段绳子捡起来——那里,我的'玩具'。"男人睁开眼睛,伸手捡起了绳子。绳子大约有两英尺(约0.6米)长,猫常常玩绳子自娱自乐,一玩就是几个小时。"现在用两只手捏住绳子的两端。"猫命令道。男人这么做了。

"你左手捏着的那端就是我的出生,而右手那端就是我的死亡。现在把两端连在一起。"猫说道。男人顺从地做了。

"你做出了一个连续不断的圆圈,"猫说,"看出这根绳子上的任意一点同其他点有什么不同吗?比绳子的其他部分更好或者更差吗?"男人审视着那根绳子,然后摇了摇头:"没有什么不同。"

"再闭上你的眼睛,"猫说,"现在舔舔你自己的手。"男人惊讶地睁大了眼睛。

"按我说的做好啦,"猫说,"舔舔你的手,想想我在我常待的地方,想想我玩过的所有绳子。"

舔自己的手,男人觉得很傻,不过他还是顺从地做了。舔着舔着,他发现了猫肯定也发现过的秘密——舔爪子能让你心静如水,让你思路变得更加清晰。他继续舔着,他的嘴角开始上扬,第一次露出了多日未见的微笑。他等待着猫叫停,可是没等到,于是他睁开了眼睛,发现猫的眼睛已经闭上了。他摩挲着猫温暖的褐色皮毛,可是猫已经去了。

男人使劲儿闭上了眼睛,泪如泉涌。他看到猫蹲在窗台上,然后是他的床上,然后躺在他的重要文件上。他看到猫在他脑袋边的枕头上,看到他明亮的金黄色眼睛,还有鼻子和耳朵上深褐色的毛发。他睁开眼睛,透过泪水看向他依然紧紧抓在手里的绳圈。

不久以后的某一天,他的膝上有了一只新的猫咪。她是一只可爱的白色花斑猫……与之前那只他深深挚爱的猫既迥然不同,又宛若一只。

The Zen of Cat

By Jim Willis

The Man was very sad. He knew that the Cat's days were numbered. The doctor had said there wasn't anything more that could be done, that he should take the Cat home and make him as comfortable as possible.

The man stroked the Cat on his lap and sighed. The Cat opened his eyes, purred and looked up at the Man. A tear rolled down the Man's cheek and landed on the Cat's forehead. The Cat gave him a slightly annoyed look.

"Why do you cry, Man?" the Cat asked. "Because you can't bear the thought of losing me? Because you think you can never replace me?" The Man nodded "yes."

"And where do you think I'll be when I leave you?" the Cat asked. The Man shrugged helplessly. "Close your eyes, Man," the Cat said. The Man gave him a questioning look, but did as he was told.

"What color are my eyes and fur?" the Cat asked. "Your

eyes are gold and your fur is a rich, warm brown," the Man replied.

"And where is it that you most often see me?" asked the Cat. "I see you…on the kitchen windowsill watching the birds…on my favorite chair…on my desk lying on the papers I need…on the pillow next to my head at night." "Then, whenever you wish to see me, all you must do is close your eyes," said the Cat.

"Pick up that piece of string from the floor—there, my 'toy'." The Man opened his eyes, then reached over and picked up the string. It was about two feet long and the Cat had been able to entertain himself for hours with it. "Now take each end of the string in one hand," the Cat ordered. The Man did so.

"The end in your left hand is my birth and the end in your right hand is my death. Now bring the two ends together," the Cat said. The Man complied.

"You have made a continuous circle," said the cat. "Does any point along the string appear to be different, worse or better than any other part of the string?" The Man inspected the string and then shook his head "no."

"Close your eyes again," the Cat said. "Now lick your hand." The Man widened his eyes in surprise.

"Just do it," the Cat said. "Lick your hand, think of me in all my familiar places, think about all the pieces of string."

The Man felt foolish, licking his hand, but he did as he was told. He discovered what a cat must know, that licking a paw is very calming and allows one to think more clearly. He continued licking and the corners of his mouth turned upward into the first smile he had shown in days. He waited for the Cat to tell him to stop, and when he didn't, he opened his eyes. The Cat's eyes were closed. The Man stroked the warm, brown fur, but the Cat was gone.

The Man shut his eyes hard as the tears poured down his face. He saw the Cat on the windowsill, then in his bed, then lying across his important papers. He saw him on the pillow next to his head, saw his bright gold eyes and darkest brown on his nose and ears. He opened his eyes and through his tears looked over at the circle of string he still held clutched in his hand.

One day, not long after, there was a new Cat on his lap. She was a lovely calico and white...very different from his earlier beloved Cat and very much the same.

泄密的心[①]

[美国]埃德加·爱伦·坡

没错儿!——我以前一直神经过敏,神经过敏得非常非常厉害,现在也是这样;可你为什么要说我疯了呢?听着!看我给你讲整个过程的时候,有多健康——有多淡定。

这念头最初是怎么钻进我的脑袋里的,我可说不来;可是一旦有了这个念头,就昼思夜想,魂牵梦绕。动机?根本没有。盛怒?根本没有,我爱那老头,他从来没有冤枉过我,他从来没有侮辱过我,我也不贪图他的金银财宝。我想是他的那只眼睛惹的祸吧!对,就是那只眼睛!他长了一只鹰眼——淡蓝色的,蒙着层薄膜。那只眼只要看我一眼,我就感到毛骨悚然;因此我心里就渐渐地——一点一点地——打定了主意,要这个老头的命,好永远地摆脱那只眼睛。

看,问题来了。你以为我疯了。疯子可是什么也不懂。只可惜你当时没看见我。只可惜你没看见我干得是多么明智——行事多么谨慎——多么有远见——我干活的时候多么会掩饰!在我杀死老头前的一个星期里,对他空前的体贴。每天晚上半夜的时候,我把他门锁一扭开——哦,多么轻手轻脚啊!接下来,我把房门拉开一条缝,宽窄正好可以探

---

① 这是一个谋杀者的忏悔(A murder's confession)。

进脑袋,就用一盏昏暗的灯塞进门缝,灯上罩得严严实实,严实得连一丝灯光都透不出来,然后我把头再伸进去。哦,你若是看见我多么巧妙地探进头去的话,一定会哈哈大笑的!我慢慢探着头——特别、特别慢,以免惊醒熟睡的老头。我花了一个小时,才把整个脑袋探进门缝,正好看见他躺在床上。哈!——难道疯子会有这样的智慧?我头一伸进房里,就小心翼翼地——哦,那么小心——小心地打开了灯罩,因为铰链会发出声音——我将灯罩掀开一条缝,这样一道细细的灯光就可以正好射在鹰眼上。我这样一连干了整整七夜——天天夜里都在午夜时分——可是我发现那只眼总是闭着;这样一来,我就下不去手,因为惹我生气的不是老头本人,而是他那只带薄膜的眼睛。

到了第八天晚上,我比往日还要小心翼翼地打开了房门。想想看,我就在房外,一点一点地打开门,可是他对于我的这种秘密行动和阴谋诡计,连做梦都没想到。想到这里,我禁不住咯咯地笑出了声;他可能是听到了,因为他仿佛大吃一惊,在床上突然翻了个身。这下你以为我会退缩了吧——可是我没有退缩。他生怕强盗抢劫,把百叶窗关得紧紧的,所以房里一片漆黑,我知道他看不见门缝,于是继续一点一点地、从容不迫地推着门。

我刚探进头,正要动手掀开灯上罩子的时候,大拇指在锡皮扣上一滑,老头一下子从床上坐起身来,大喊一声:"谁在那里?"

我一动不动,一声不吭。整整一个小时,我连肌肉都没动一下,与此同时,我也没听到他躺下的声音。

不久,我听到了一声轻轻的呻吟,我知道只有恐惧至极才会这么呻吟。既不是痛苦的呻吟,也不是悲叹——哦,不是!——那是在吓得魂飞魄散时,不由自主地从心灵深处发出的、低低的呻吟。我倒是对这种声音心领神会。我知道他刚刚听到轻微的那声响动，在床上翻身以后，就一直大睁着双眼躺着。他心里的恐惧在逐渐升级。他一直在安慰自己这是一场虚惊，却一直没能奏效。

我非常耐心地等了好长时间，始终没有听到他躺下的声音，于是决定将灯罩掀开一条小缝，极小、极小的一道缝。我动手掀开灯罩——你可能想象不出，有多么、多么鬼鬼祟祟，——最后终于射出了一道微弱的光，仿佛蛛丝，从那道缝里射出，照在了鹰眼上。

那只眼睁着呢——睁得好大、好大。我一看，不禁怒火中烧。我看得一清二楚——整个眼睛只是一团暗淡的蓝，蒙着一层可怕的薄膜，让我毛骨悚然，不寒而栗。可是，我却看不见老头的脸庞和身体，因为我凭着直觉，让灯光正好射在那只鬼眼睛上了。

此时，我耳边传来低沉的、单调的、短促的声音，就好像把一块表包裹在布里发出的声音。我对这种声音也很熟悉。这是老头的心跳声。我的火气更大了，如同士兵听到了战鼓咚咚，士气大增一样。

即便在此时，我依然克制着自己，纹丝不动。我连大气都不喘一下。我提着灯，一动不动。我让灯光尽量稳稳地射在鹰眼上。与此同时，吓人的、扑通扑通的心跳声越来越大了。一秒比一秒快，一秒比一秒大。老头的恐惧一定已经到了极限！我说，心跳声越来越大，一秒钟比一秒钟大！你听明白了没有？我早就告诉过你，我神经过敏；我确实神经过敏。此刻正是鸦雀无声的午夜时分，古屋里一片死寂，耳听得这种古怪的声音，让我不由自主地毛骨悚然。可是几分钟后，我依然克制着自己，纹丝不动地站着。然而心跳声竟然愈来愈大，愈来愈大！我猜，那颗心一定是要爆炸了。

此时，我又产生了一种新的焦虑——邻居恐怕会听到这心跳声！老头的死期到啦！我大吼一声，扯开灯罩，跳进屋里。他尖叫了一声——只叫了那么一声。就在那一刹那,我一把把他拖到地板上,把沉重的大床压在他身上。接下来,看到已经万事大吉,我开心地笑了。可是,几分钟过去了,闷声闷气的心跳声还在响个不停。这倒也没惹我生气,墙外是听不见的。后来终于没动静了。老头死了。我把床挪开,审视着尸体。我把手放在他胸口,停留了好几分钟。心脏不再跳动了。他死透了。那只眼睛再也不会惹我烦了。

你还当我发疯的话,等我给你讲讲我藏匿尸体所采取的明智的预防措施,你就不会这么想了。夜色阑珊,我要抓紧时间干,却不能弄出动静来。我先将尸首肢解开来。

然后,我再撬起屋里的三块地板,将肢解后的尸体都藏在两根间柱当中。接下来,我把木板归位,干得那么巧妙、那么机智。人的眼睛都看不出有丝毫破绽——就连他的眼睛也看不出。

大功告成,一切就绪,已经四点钟了——夜色沉沉,如同子夜。钟表报时,临街的大门外传来一阵敲门声。我心情愉快地下楼去开门,——我现在还有什么好怕的呢?门外进来了三个人,他们做了自我介绍说是警官,绝对的和颜悦色。有个街坊在夜里听到一声尖叫,疑心出了不轨之事,报了警,这三位警官就奉命前来搜查楼里的各户人家了。

我满脸堆笑——有什么好怕的呢?我对这三位警官表示欢迎。我说,那声尖叫是我刚才做梦时发出的。我提到老头不在家,到乡下去了。我带着三位来客在家里上上下下走了个遍。我请他们搜查——仔细搜查。最后我还领着他们进了老头的卧房,指给他们看他的家私都完好无损,原封没动。我心里有谱,还热情洋溢地搬进几把椅子,请他们在这间房里歇脚,与此同时,我自鸣得意,还胆大包天地搬了把椅子,专门在埋着冤鬼尸体的地方坐了下来。

警官们心满意足了。我的所作所为令他们心悦诚服。我也异常轻松自在。可是没过多久,我就觉得自己脸色越来越苍白,恨不得他们马上离开。我头痛欲裂,还觉得耳朵里嗡嗡地响;可是他们仍坐着,还在东拉西扯。嗡嗡声更清楚了;嗡嗡声在继续,听起来越发清楚了;我最后终于发现原来声音不是来自耳朵里。

不消说,我此时的脸色已经特别苍白了,可我的话说得更溜了,嗓门儿也提高了。可那嗡嗡声越来越大——我该如何是好呢?这是一种低沉的、模糊的、短促的声音——就像包裹在棉布里的一块表发出的声音。我开始气喘吁吁了——可是这三位警官竟然没听到。我说话的语速更快了——情绪更热烈了,可是响声却在持续增大。他们为什么还不走呢?我拖着沉重的脚步在房里踱来踱去,好像被这些人的监视激怒一般,可响声还在持续增大。哦,上帝啊!我该如何是好呢?我唾沫星子四溅——我胡言乱语——我破口大骂!我摇晃自己的座椅,在木板上摩擦,可是那个响声却盖过所有的声音,还在持续增大。那个响声越来越大——越来越大——越来越大。可是那三个人还在愉快地东拉西扯,嘻嘻哈哈。难道他们听不见吗?

他们听见了!——他们怀疑了!——他们知道真相了!——他们正在嘲笑我这样吓破了胆呢!——我刚才是这么想的,现在还是这么想。可怎么着都比这种痛苦好忍受!怎么着都比这种嘲笑好受!我再也受不了这种皮笑肉不笑啦!我觉得再不尖叫就要死了!——听啊——又来了!——我听到那响声越来越大!越来越大!越来越大!越来越大!

"坏蛋!"我大声尖叫,"别装啦!我认罪!——撬开地板!这里!这里!——是他那颗可恶的心的跳动声!"

The Tell-Tale Heart

By Edgar Allan Poe

True!—nervous—very, very dreadfully nervous I had been and am; but why will you say that I am mad? Hearken! And observe how healthily—how calmly I can tell you the whole story.

It is impossible to say how first the idea entered my brain; but once conceived, it haunted me day and night. Object, there was none. Passion, there was none. I loved the old man. He had never wronged me. He had never given me insult. For his gold I had no desire. I think it was his eye! Yes, it was this! One of his eyes resembled that of a vulture—a pale blue eye, with a film over it. Whenever it fell upon me, my blood ran cold; and so by degrees—very gradually—I made up my mind to take the life of the old man, and thus rid my life of him forever.

Now, this is the point. You fancy me mad. Madmen know nothing. But you should have seen me. You should have seen how wisely I proceeded—with what caution—with what foresight—with what dissimulation I went to work! I was never kinder to the old man than during the whole week before I killed him. And every night, about midnight, I turned the latch of his door and opened it—oh, so gently! And then, when I had made an opening sufficient for my head, I put in a dark lantern, all closed, closed so that no light shone out, and then I thrust in my head. Oh, you would have laughed to see how cunningly I thrust it in! I moved it slowly—very, very slowly, so that I might not disturb the old man's sleep. It took me an hour to place my whole head within the opening so far that I could see him as he lay upon the bed. Ha! — would a madman have been so wise as this? And then, when my head was well in the room, I undid the lantern cautiously—oh, so cautiously—cautiously (for the hinges creaked) I undid it just so much that a single thin ray fell upon the vulture eye. And this I did for seven long nights—every night just at midnight—but I found the eye always closed; and so it was impossible to do the work; for it was not the old man who vexed me, but his evil eye.

Upon the eighth night I was more than usually cautious in opening the door. To think that there I was, opening the door, little by little, and he not even to dream of my secret deeds or thoughts. I fairly chuckled at the idea; and perhaps he heard me; for he moved on the bed suddenly, as if startled. Now you may think that I drew back—but no. His room was as black as pitch with the thick darkness (for the shutters were close fastened, through fear of robbers), and so I knew that he could not see the opening of the door, and I kept pushing it on steadily, steadily.

I had my head in, and was about to open the lantern, when my thumb slipped upon the tin fastening, and the old man sprang up in the bed crying out—"Who's there?"

I kept quite still and said nothing. For a whole hour I did not move a muscle, and in the meantime I did not hear him lie down.

Presently I heard a slight groan, and I knew it was the groan of mortal terror. It was not a groan of pain or of grief—oh, no!—it was the low, stifled sound that arises from the bottom of the soul when overcharged with awe. I knew the sound well. I knew that he had been lying awake ever since the first slight noise, when he had turned in the bed. His fears had been ever since growing upon him. He had been trying to fancy them causeless, but could not.

When I had waited a long time, very patiently, without hearing him lie down, I resolved to open a little—a very, very little crevice in the lantern. So I opened it—you cannot imagine how stealthily, stealthily—until at length a single dim ray, like the thread of the spider, shot from out the crevice and fell upon the vulture eye.

It was open—wide, wide open—and I grew furious as I gazed upon it. I saw it with perfect distinctness—all a dull blue, with a hideous veil over it that chilled the very marrow in my bones; but I could see nothing else of the old man's face or person; for I had directed the ray as if by instinct, precisely upon the spot.

Now, there came to my ears a low, dull, quick sound, such as a watch makes when enveloped in cotton. I knew that sound well, too. It was the beating of the old man's heart. It increased my fury, as the beating of a drum stimulates the soldier into courage.

But even yet I refrained and kept still. I scarcely breathed; I held the lantern motionless. I tried how steadily I could maintain the ray upon the eye. Meantime the hellish tattoo of the heart increased. It grew quicker and quicker, and louder and louder every instant. The old man's terror must have been extreme! It grew louder, I say, louder every moment! Do you mark me well? I have told you that I am nervous; so I am. And now at the dead hour of the night, amid the dreadful silence of that old house, so strange a noise as this excited me to uncontrollable terror. Yet for some minutes longer I refrained and stood still. But the beating grew louder, louder! I thought the heart must burst.

And now a new anxiety seized me—the sound could be heard by a neighbour! The old man's hour had come! With a loud yell I threw open the lantern and leaped into the room. He shrieked once—once only. In an instant I dragged him to the floor, and pulled the heavy bed over him. I then smiled gaily to find the deed so far done. But for many minutes the heart beat on with a muffled sound. This, however, did not vex me; it would not be heard through the wall. At length it ceased. The old man was dead. I removed the bed and examined the corpse. I placed my hand upon the heart and held it there many minutes. There was no pulsation.

He was stone dead. His eye would trouble me no more.

If you still think me mad, you will think so no longer when I describe the wise precautions I took for the concealment of the body. The night waned, and I worked hastily, but in silence. First of all I dismembered the corpse.

I then took up three planks from the flooring of the chamber and deposited all between the scantlings. I then replaced the boards so cleverly, so cunningly, that no human eye—not even his—could have detected anything wrong.

When I had made an end of these labors, it was four o'clock—still dark as midnight. As the bell sounded the hour, there came a knocking at the street door. I went down to open it with a light heart—for what had I now to fear? Then entered three men who introduced themselves, with perfect suavity, as officers of the police. A shriek had been heard by a neighbor during the night; suspicion of foul play had been aroused; information had been lodged at the police office, and the officers had been deputed to search the premises.

I smiled—for what had I to fear? I bade the gentlemen welcome. The shriek, I said, was my own in a dream. The old man, I mentioned, was absent in the country. I took my visitors all over the house. I bade them search—search well. I led them at length to his chamber. I showed them his treasures, secure, undisturbed. In the enthusiasm of my confidence I brought chairs into the room, and desired them here to rest from their fatigues, while I myself, in the wild audacity of my perfect triumph, placed my own seat upon the very spot beneath which reposed the corpse of the victim.

The officers were satisfied. My manner had convinced them. I was singularly at ease. But ere long I felt myself getting pale and wished them gone. My head ached, and I fancied a ringing in my ears; but still they sat and still chatted. The ringing became more distinct; it continued and gained definitiveness—until at length I found that the noise was not within my ears.

No doubt I grew very pale; but I talked more fluently and with a heightened voice. Yet the sound increased—and what could I do? It was a low, dull, quick sound—much such a sound as a watch makes when enveloped in cotton. I gasped for breath—and yet the officers heard it not. I talked more quickly—more vehemently; but the noise steadily increased. Why would they not be gone? I paced the floor to and fro with heavy strides, as if excited to fury by the observations of the men—but the noise steadily increased. O God! what could I do? I foamed—I raved—I swore! I swung the chair upon which I had been sitting, and grated it upon the boards, but the noise arose over all and continually increased. It grew louder—louder—louder. And still the men chatted pleasantly and smiled. Was it possible they heard not?

They heard!—They suspected!—They knew!—They were making a mockery of my horror! This I thought and this I think.

But anything was better than this agony! Anything was more tolerable than this derision! I could bear those hypocritical smiles no longer! I felt that I must scream or die! —and now—again! —hark I louder! Louder! Louder! Louder!

"Villains!" I shrieked, "Dissemble no more! I admit the deed—tear up the planks! Here! Here! It is the beating of his hideous heart!"

希望与安慰

[美国] A.J. 麦肯纳

查理·弗利到美国国立大学医院看望他的妻子多莉。

"你感觉怎么样?"他边问边坐到了床边,靠近对着他微笑的多莉,她的黑发靠在白色枕头上。

"我很好。"多莉平静地说。在查理看来,她看上去苍老疲惫,脸色惨白,眼睛下面有黑色的眼袋。当她把手指伸进查理手指间时,他注意到她的小手背上有两个难看的褐色斑点。

"你看起来很疲惫。"查理说,"你没睡觉吧?"

"我昨晚有点焦躁不安。"

多莉没有提到痛苦:她不想让她丈夫难过。

"琳达有什么消息吗?"她问。

"她昨晚又打来电话,我告诉她你很了不起,我说没什么好担心的。"

琳达,他们最大的孩子,在戈尔韦的一所大学教书。琳达将在8月回家度假。他们的儿子科姆和他的孩子住在澳大利亚。他们没有告诉科姆他的母亲身体不好。科姆是个爱忧心忡忡的人:最好不要让他心烦意乱。

查理在喧闹的医院病房里凝望着，心不在焉。下午的阳光淡淡的、亮亮的。其他探视者也在尽他们的义务，聚集在病人周围，带来鲜花和水果，说着带有希望和安慰的话语。

"你又见医生了吗？"查理问他妻子。

"可能明天会。"

"你知道他们会把你留多久吗？"

多莉转过身，对着一张纸巾咳嗽，然后转回来。她再次握住了查理的手。

"他们星期一会告诉我的。他们必须做更多的检查。直到他们了解以后才会让我回家。很抱歉，我太麻烦了。"

多莉干瘪的胸部在厚重的睡衣下面起伏着。这让查理想到了一只受惊吓的鸟。亲爱的多洛丽丝·德拉罗萨，很久以前，他们在取悦对方的时候就是这样叫她的，取笑她悲伤的眼睛，嘲笑她对待一切太认真的方式。他不禁纳闷起来，她是否是因担心而生的病呢？

可怜的多莉·德拉罗萨！

他说："在你完全好转之前，不要让他们改变你的想法。"

"你还好吗，亲爱的？"

"很好。"

查理在外面吃饭，尽量远离家。他把自己打理得很好。

在闷热和乏味中，时间一分钟一分钟地过去。查理看着来访者，瞥了一眼他妻子床边的小闹钟。他能听到远处嘀嗒作响的声音，还记得黎明时分把妻子从床上拽下来的恼人的铃声。过了一会儿，她在厨房里做早餐发出叮叮当当的声音，吵得他无法入睡，让他想起还有一天的工作要做，还要喂孩子吃饭，送孩子们上学。

嘀嗒——嘀嗒——嘀嗒——嘀嗒——嘀嗒——嘀嗒——嘀嗒。

孩子们都长大了。第二个孙子即将出生。时间不多了。剃须镜中一张灰色的脸提醒查理自己已经人到中年,即将老去。如果你不能享受的话,有钱又有什么意义呢?为什么钟不能慢慢走?走得怎么这么急?

啊——上帝保佑你!多莉·多洛罗萨。没有她会有什么不同?

多莉的眼皮下垂。她的嘴张开了一部分。她看起来快死了。时间缓缓流逝。

"这对你来说一定很无聊吧。"她闭着眼睛说。

"一点儿也不。见到你真好。"

"去医院看望病人可不是件好事,太令人沮丧了。"

"瞎说。"

多莉把她黑色的头部往后靠在白色枕头上。有那么一瞬间,她面容扭曲,然后勇敢地一笑。

"你该走了,查理,我想睡一会儿。"

"真的?"

"真的。"

查理跳了起来。

他说:"我晚点再来。"

"求你今天不要来了。明天是星期六,病房里一定会挤满了人。会持续一上午。你做完弥撒再来吧。"

"这就是你希望的吗?"

"是的,亲爱的。"

多莉睁开眼睛,笑得像个孩子。多莉很久没当孩子了。

"你看起来很疲惫,亲爱的,"她说,"你没睡好吗?"

"我昨晚有点心神不宁。"

"试着放松一下。"

多莉捏着丈夫的手,戴指环的手指按在他的金婚戒指上。她的手指像羽毛一样轻。

"你走吧,亲爱的,"她说,"尽量别担心。"

查理弯下腰,亲吻多莉滚烫的额头。

"我明天再来看你。"他说。

多莉的眼睛闭上了。她的手指从他的手上滑了下来。

嘀嗒——嘀嗒——嘀嗒——嘀嗒——嘀嗒。

查理沿着一条光滑的走廊走着,找到了出口。在外面明亮的停车场里,他找到了自己的车,坐了进去。他环顾四周来来往往的来客。护士走过,让他想起了蝴蝶。查理伸手拿起他的手机,拨了一个号码。电话几乎马上就被接通了。

"凯瑟琳?"他说。

"你在哪儿?我等你的电话很久了。"

"我在医院外面,我刚来看过她。"

"她怎么样?"

"好吧。可以预料的好,我想。但谁真的知道呢?"

查理拉下遮光板,以保护他的眼睛不受眩目阳光的伤害,然后他的注意力回到他的新朋友——凯瑟琳身上。

"她还会有一段时间。"

"待会儿见吗?"凯瑟琳问。

"我希望如此。"

"今晚别走,"她说,"如果你愿意的话。"

查理想到了自己空荡荡的房子,没有多莉的宁静,以及她留下的可怕的沉默。

"我愿意,亲爱的。"他说。

"来吧。"凯瑟琳轻声说道,声音里带着发自内心的笑意。"我会让你高兴起来的。"

查理说再见,把电话收起来。那天他第一次真正地笑了。他发动引擎,当他驱车离开时,查理透过后视镜瞥了一眼,看到灰色的医院大楼像监狱一样后退。

上帝帮助我,他想。上帝帮助我们所有人。

Hope and Comfort

By A. J. McKenna

Charley Foley calls into the Mater Misericordia Hospital to visit his wife.

"How are you feeling?" he asks, sitting at the bedside, close to Dolly who is smiling up at him, her black hair resting against the white pillows.

"I'm fine," Dolly says, quietly. She looks old and tired to Charley; she is deathly pale and has black pouches under her eyes. When she slips her fingers into Charley's he notices two ugly brown liver spots on the back her small hand.

"You look tired," Charley says. "Aren't you sleeping?"

"I was a bit restless last night."

Dolly does not mention the pain: she doesn't want to upset her husband.

"Any word from Linda?" she asks.

"She phoned again last night. I told her you were grand. I said there was nothing to worry about."

Linda, their eldest, teaches in a university in Galway. Linda will come home for the holiday in August. Their son, Colm, and his children live in Australia. Colm hasn't been told that his mother is unwell. Colm's a worrier: it's best he's not upset.

Charley gazes dreamily across the chattering hospital ward, bright with pale afternoon sunlight. Other visitors are doing their duties, gathering around the sick, bringing flowers and fruit, offering words of hope and comfort.

"Have you seen the doctor again?" Charley asks his wife.

"Tomorrow maybe."

"Any idea how long they'll keep you in?"

Dolly turns away and coughs into a tissue, then settles back. She takes Charley's hand again.

"They'll let me know on Monday. They have to do lots more tests. They won't let me home until they know. I'm sorry to be such a bother."

Dolly's small chest heaves under her heavy nightdress. Charley thinks of a frightened bird. Sweet Dolores Delarosa he used to call her long ago when they were courting, mocking her sorrowful eyes and the way she took everything too seriously. He can't help wondering if she made herself sick with worry.

Poor Dolly Delarosa!

"Don't let them budge you until you're absolutely better," he says.

"Are you managing all right, darling?"

"Grand."

Charley is eating out and staying away from the house as much as possible. He's managing all right.

The minutes pass in heated tedium. Charley is watching the visitors and glancing at the small alarm clock beside his wife's bed. He can hear its distant ticking and still recall the irritating ring when it dragged his wife from bed at the crack of dawn and moments later her breakfast sounds clattering in the kitchen keeping him awake, reminding him that there's a day's work ahead and children to be schooled and fed.

Tic–tic–tic–tic–tic–tic–tic.

The kids are all grown up now. Second grandchild imminent. Time is running out. A grey face in the shaving mirror reminding Charley of middle age and the rot ahead. Where's the point in having money if you can't enjoy it? Why can't clocks take their time? What's the hurry?

Ah—God have mercy! Dolly Dolorosa. How different might it have been without her?

Dolly's eyelids droop. Her mouth opens a fraction. She looks almost dead. Moments pass slowly.

"This must be very boring for you," she says, without opening her eyes.

"Not at all. It does me good to see you."

"It's not nice having to visit anybody in hospital. It's so depressing."

"Nonsense."

Dolly settles her dark head further back against the white pillows. Grimaces for an instant then braves a smile.

"You should leave now, Charley. I think I might sleep for a while."

"Are you sure?"

"Positive."

Charley bounces to his feet.

"I'll come in later," he says.

"Please don't. With it being Saturday the wards will be crammed with people. Leave it till the morning. Come after Mass."

"Is that's what you want?"

"It is, darling."

Dolly opens her eyes, smiles like a child. It's been a long time since Dolly was a child.

"You look tired, darling," she says. "Aren't you sleeping?"

"I was a bit restless last night."

"Try to take things easy."

Dolly squeezes her husband's hand, presses her ringed finger against his gold wedding ring. Her fingers are light as feathers.

"Off you go, darling," she says. "Try to not worry."

Charley bends and kisses Dolly's hot forehead.

"I'll see you tomorrow," he says.

Dolly's eyes close. Her fingers slip from his.

Tic–tic–tic–tic–tic.

Charley walks along a polished corridor and finds the exit. Outside in the bright car park he locates his car and sits inside. He glances around at the visitors coming and going. Nurses walk past, reminding him of butterflies. Charley reaches for his mobile phone and taps in a number. The call is answered almost immediately.

"Katherine?" he says.

"Where are you? I've been waiting ages for you to call."

"I'm outside the hospital. I've just been in to see her."

"How is she?"

"All right. As well as can be expected, I suppose. Who really knows?"

Charley pulls down the sunshade to protect his eyes from the blinding brightness, then returns his attention to his new friend, Katherine.

"She'll be in for a while longer."

"Will I see you later?" Katherine asks.

"I expect so."

"Stay tonight," she offers. "If you like."

Charley thinks of his own empty house, the quietness without Dolly and the dreadful silences she left behind.

"I'd like that, darling," he says.

"Come now," Katherine whispers with a smile in her lovely voice. "I'll cheer you up."

Charley says goodbye and puts the phone away. He smiles properly for the first time that day. He starts the engine and as he drives away Charley glances through the rear view mirror and sees the grey hospital building receding like a prison.

God help me, he thinks. God help us all.

老 鼠

[英国] 萨基

西奥多里克·沃勒的母亲是一位慈母。在母亲的关怀下,西奥多里克从小到大都远离着母亲口中的"粗糙的现实生活"。母亲去世后,他不得不开始独自面对这个比他想象的还要粗糙许多的世界。对他来说,即使是一次简单的搭乘火车的旅行都充满了琐碎小事的烦恼。今天是9月的一个早晨,当他在一个二等座车厢内坐下以后,他的情绪就一直是焦躁不安的。

此前,他一直在朋友的农场度假。农场的主人是一位教区牧师,他有一个女儿。这父女俩人都很好,但西奥多里克还是觉得在这里的日子比他之前已经习惯了的更混乱。因此,回家时能够坐上那架小马车去火车站都会给他带来前所未有的、井然有序的感觉,而当离去的时刻临近时,这架马车并没有出现在他的视线里。

在这样的紧急情况下,令西奥多里克厌恶的是,他发现自己要与牧师的女儿合作从邻居的马厩弄来一架小马车,那个马厩里有一股老鼠的味道。西奥多里克其实并不怕老鼠,只不过把老鼠视为生活中的粗糙之物。牧师的女儿提出要用邻居家的马和车把他送到火车站,他欣然接受了。他及时赶到了火车站,并在自己的车厢里安顿了下来。

火车驶出车站时,西奥多里克的内心已经烦躁起来。车厢是那种老式布局,因此在这样的共用车厢里,西奥多里克的一半隐私可以很好地通过座椅间的过道得到保护。然而,当火车差不多提到正常车速后,他清楚地意识到自己并不是一个人,车厢另一侧还坐着一位沉睡的女士,甚至连他的衣服里都不止他一个人。

他感到身上有个暖暖的东西在爬,然后发现这个"不速之客"是一只不受欢迎、让他深恶痛绝的老鼠,应该是在他去马厩牵马时闯进他衣服里的。一阵疯狂的跺脚和摇晃身体并没有赶走这个入侵者,它似乎挺愿意留在他的衣服里。令人无法想象的是,他还得在这列火车上忍受着这些在他衣服里到处游荡的老鼠整整一个小时(在他的想象里,侵入他衣服里的老鼠数量至少是实际的两倍)。而直接脱掉衣服会让他瞬间摆脱这种折磨。可是当着一位女士的面脱掉衣服,虽然这位女士在睡觉,这想法本身就会羞得他耳尖火辣辣的,满脸绯红。

然而,此时此刻,这位女士睡梦正酣;而这只老鼠似乎在他的衣服里很是享受。有时,它会滑倒,然后被吓了一跳,或者更可能的是来了火气,张口就咬。西奥多里克绝望了。他的脸红得像个甜菜根,同时极度痛苦地注视着他的这位酣睡的旅伴。然后,他以最快的速度脱下了自己的衣服,打算把那只老鼠从衣服里弄出来。

就在他脱衣服的时候,老鼠猛地跳到地板上,吓得西奥多里克失声尖叫,尖叫声太大了,那位沉睡的旅伴被惊醒了,睁开了眼睛。西奥多里克用比那只老鼠更快的动作抓起了自己的衣服,挡在了自己身前,然后跳到车厢最远处的角落里。然而,这位女士凝视着她面前这位陌生的旅伴,自娱自乐。她都看到了什么?西奥多里克问自己。无论如何,她现在会怎么想他?

"我想我是感冒了。"他绝望地说。"真是对不起。"她回答,"我只是想问您是否可以打开这扇窗子。我的包里有一些白兰地,如果您能帮忙把包递给我,我会给您一些,喝点会有用的。"他的这位旅伴说。"不用了,不用了。"他安慰她说。他想知道是否可以直接把真相告诉她?"您怕老鼠吗?"他开口说道,脸变得似乎比之前更红了,如果还能更红的话。"还好,别一大群就行。你为什么问这个?""刚刚有一只在我的衣服里爬来着,"西奥多里克用几乎不像他本人的声音说,"这种情况非常尴尬。"

"老鼠有奇怪的舒适理念。""我不得不在您睡觉时把它弄出来。"他继续说。然后,他叹了口气,补充道:"我把它弄出来了,但是这个过程就要结束时,我成了……现在的样子。""当然,把老鼠弄出来不会引起感冒的。"她说。很显然,对于西奥多里克面临的困境,她还挺享受的。

羞辱的感觉被纯粹的恐惧所取代。随着时间的流逝,火车正越来越靠近人头攒动的终点站。他还剩下一个小小的机会——在火车到站前重新穿上衣服。他的这位旅伴可能会继续睡觉。

可是,随着时间一分一秒地过去,这样的机会也随之变得越来越小。她仍然睡意全无。"我想我们现在肯定是要到站了。"她说。西奥多里克已经注意到旅程的终点即将到来,他内心的恐惧感也随之越来越强烈。"您可不可以,"她问,"帮我找一个行李搬运工,把我的行李搬到出租车上?很不好意思在您感觉不舒服时给您添麻烦,但双目失明让我在上下火车时感到很无助。"

The Mouse

By SAKI

Theodoric Voler had been brought up by a loving mother whose main focus had been to keep him away from what she called "the coarser realities of life". When she died she left Theodoric alone in a world that was a good deal coarser than he thought it had any need to be. To him, even a simple railway journey was full with petty annoyances, and as he sat down in a second-class compartment one September morning he was having ruffled feelings.

He had been staying as a vacation at a farm owned by family friends; a vicar and his daughter. They were nice people, but more chaotic than he was used to. So when it was time for him to return home, the pony carriage that was to take him to the station had never been properly ordered, and when the moment for his departure drew near, the carriage was nowhere in sight.

In this emergency Theodoric, to his disgust, found himself collaborating with the vicar's daughter in the task of getting a pony carriage from the neighbours' stable, where it smelled of mice. Without being actually afraid of mice, Theodoric saw mice as one of the coarser incidents of life. The daughter offered to take him to the station with the pony and carriage of her neighbours, which he gladly accepted. He made it in time and settled himself in his compartment.

As the train rolled out of the station, Theodoric became bored already. The carriage was of the old-fashioned sort, so that Theodoric's semi privacy in his shared compartment was protected well by corridors. And yet the train had barely reached its normal speed before he became vividly aware that he was not alone with a slumbering lady sitting on the other side of his train compartment; he was not even alone in his own clothes.

A warm, creeping movement over his body revealed the unwelcome and highly resented presence of a mouse, that had dashed into his clothes when he was getting the pony. Wild stamps and shakes failed to get rid of the intruder, who seemingly wished to stay in his clothes. It was unthinkable that he should continue a whole hour on the train being a house for wandering mice (already his imagination had at least doubled the numbers of the mouse invasion). On the other hand, simply taking off his clothes would release him from his tormentor instantly. Yet, to undress in the presence of a lady, even though she was sleeping, was an idea that made his ear tips tingle in a blush of shame.

And yet—the lady in this case was soundly asleep; the mouse, on the other hand, seemed to be enjoying himself a lot inside his clothes. Sometimes it slipped and then, in fright, or more probably temper, it bit. Theodoric was desperate. Turning red as a beetroot and keeping an agonised watch on his slumbering fellow traveller, he swiftly hasted to undress himself and remove the mouse from his clothes.

As he took his clothes off, the mouse gave a wild leap to the floor, making Theodoric scream with fear, so loud that the sleeper opened her eyes. With a movement almost quicker than the mouse's, Theodoric grabbed his clothes, pushed them in front of himself and jumped into the farthest corner of the compartment. The lady, however, entertained herself with a silent stare at her strange companion. How much had she seen? Theodoric asked himself; and in any case what on earth must she think of him now?

"I think I have caught a cold," he said desperately. "Really, I'm sorry," she replied. "I was just going to ask you if you could open this window. I've got some brandy in my bag, if you'll kindly give me my bag I will give you some, it will help." said his companion. "Not needed, not needed." he assured her. Would it be possible, he wondered, to simply tell her the truth? "Are you afraid of mice?" he started, growing, if possible, more red in the face. "Not unless they came in large groups. Why do you ask?" "I had one crawling inside my clothes just now," said Theodoric in a voice that hardly seemed his own. "It was a very awkward situation."

"Mice do have strange ideas of comfort." "I had to get rid of it while you were asleep," he continued. Then, with a sigh, he added, "I got rid of it, but in the process I ended up like… this." "Surely getting rid of a mouse wouldn't cause a cold," she said. Clearly she was enjoying his confusion.

Sheer terror took the place of his humiliation. With every minute that passed the train was rushing nearer to the crowded end destination. There was one tiny chance he could still put his clothes back on before they arrived: his fellow traveller might continue to sleep.

But as the minutes passed by, that chance ebbed away. She remained very much awake. "I think we must be getting near now," she said. Theodoric had already noted with growing terror the journey's end was about to come. "Would you be so kind," she asked, "to get me a porter to take me to a cab? It's a shame to trouble you when you're feeling unwell, but being blind makes me so helpless at a railway station."

不舒服的床

[法国] 居伊·德·莫泊桑

秋天的时候,我和一些朋友留在庇卡底的一座城堡里等待狩猎季。

我的朋友们喜欢搞恶作剧,我所有的朋友都是这样,我也不愿意结识其他类型的人。

他们隆重地欢迎我的到来,这样的举动让我心生疑窦。我们之前也有过一些真正的狩猎。他们拥抱我,哄着我,好像他们要捉弄我寻开心似的。

我心里想:"小心点,老雪貂!他们可是有预谋的。"

晚饭的时候,笑语喧哗,实际上是闹翻了天。我想:"这里有一些人没缘由地异常兴奋。他们一定是在自己的脑海里设计了一些有趣的笑料。我肯定会成为这些笑话的受害者。要当心!"

整个晚上,每个人都笑得非常夸张。我闻到空气里弥漫着恶作剧的味道,正如狗闻到狩猎的味道一样。但这是什么恶作剧呢?我小心提防着,坐立不安起来。我没有错过他们说的每一个词,透露的每一个意思,做的每一个动作。在我看来,每个人都是被怀疑的对象,我甚至不信任地看着仆人们的脸。

该上床睡觉了,大家把我送到房间。为什么?

他们对我大声说:"晚安。"我进了房间关上门,站在门口,手里拿着一支蜡烛,一步也没挪。

我听到走廊里传来笑声和窃窃私语。毫无疑问,他们一定正在偷窥我。我朝墙扫视了一圈,家具、天花板、挂件、地板。没什么可疑的地方。我听门外的脚步声,毫无疑问,他们一定在通过猫眼向里面看。

我想到了一个点子:"突然吹灭蜡烛,让自己置身在一片漆黑中。"

然后我走到壁炉台,点燃了上面所有的蜡烛。之后又向四周扫了一眼,还是没有发现什么。我向前踱了一小步,仔细检查这个房间。什么可疑的东西都没有。我一件件地检查着房间里的物品,还是没有发现可疑之处。我走到窗边,看到木质大百叶窗敞开着。我小心翼翼地把窗户关上,把大大的天鹅绒窗帘拉上,拉了把椅子坐在窗前,这样就没什么可害怕的了。

我小心谨慎地坐下,扶手椅很牢固。我不会冒险上床去。然而,时间过得很快,我最终得出的结论是我真是荒唐可笑。假如他们正在像我推测的那样偷看我的话,他们一定在等着看为我准备的恶作剧的效果,一直在笑话我胆小如鼠。所以我决定上床。但是床看起来特别可疑。我拉起窗帘,看起来很安全。

尽管如此,我还是觉得有危险。我可能会发现冷水当头而下,或者可能刚在床上伸展四肢就发现自己跟床垫一起掉到地上。我在记忆里搜寻我所经历过的那些恶作剧。我不想再次中招。啊!当然不想!肯定不想!我想到了一种极端有效的防范措施:我小心翼翼地抓着床垫一侧,慢慢拉向自己。床垫包括床单和其他东西一起被拉了过来。我把这些东西拉到房间的正中,面朝门的方向。我尽可能地重新整理出一个临时床铺,与那个可疑的床架和让我感到那么焦虑不安的角落保持距离。然后我吹灭所有蜡烛,摸索着溜到床铺所在的位置,钻进被窝。

至少有一个小时，我都没睡，听见一点点声响就惊恐不安。城堡里的一切都安静下来。我睡着了。

我一定熟睡了很久，却突然被一个重重的身体砸中，惊醒过来。与此同时，我感觉脸上、脖子上、胸上都有烫人的液体，疼得我大声号叫。一阵可怕的声音，好像餐柜里的盘子和碟子纷纷掉落，刺穿我的耳膜。

我感觉到自己被压在砸下来的那个重物下面动弹不得，快要窒息了。我伸出手想摸摸是什么东西。我摸到了一张脸、一个鼻子，还有胡须。我使出浑身力气朝这张脸打了一拳。但立刻感觉有什么东西像冰雹似的掉下来，我立即从那湿透的床单上跳出来，穿着睡衣跑到走廊，我发现门是开着的。

噢！太蠢了！光天化日之下能有这样的怪事。嘈杂声是我的朋友们进公寓时发出的，我们发现，倒在我临时床铺上的是家里一脸惊愕的仆人。原来他给我送早餐的时候，被地板中间的障碍物绊倒，摔了个大马趴，身不由己的他把早餐洒了我一脸。

关窗，把临时床铺搭在房间中间这些预防措施是我努力避害的小插曲。

啊！他们那天笑了整整一天！

An Uncomfortable Bed

By Guy de Maupassant

One autumn I went to spend the hunting season with some friends in a chateau in Picardy.

My friends were fond of practical jokes. I do not care to know people who are not.

When I arrived, they gave me a princely reception, which at once awakened suspicion in my mind. They fired off rifles, embraced me, made much of me, as if they expected to have great fun at my expense.

I said to myself: "Look out, old ferret! They have something in store for you."

During the dinner the mirth was excessive, exaggerated, in fact. I thought: "Here are people who have more than their share of amusement, and apparently without reason. They must have planned some good joke. Assuredly I am to be the victim of the joke. Attention!"

During the entire evening everyone laughed in an exaggerated fashion. I scented a practical joke in the air, as a dog scents game. But what was it? I was watchful, restless. I did not let a word, or a meaning, or a gesture escape me. Everyone seemed to me an object of suspicion, and I even looked distrustfully at the faces of the servants.

The hour struck for retiring; and the whole household came to escort me to my room. Why?

They called to me: "Good-night." I entered the apartment, shut the door, and remained standing, without moving a single step, holding the wax candle in my hand.

I heard laughter and whispering in the corridor. Without doubt they were spying on me. I cast a glance round the walls, the furniture, the ceiling, the hangings, the floor. I saw nothing to justify suspicion. I heard persons moving about outside my door. I had no doubt they were looking through the keyhole.

An idea came into my head: "My candle may suddenly go out and leave me in darkness."

Then I went across to the mantelpiece and lighted all the wax candles that were on it. After that I cast another glance around me without discovering anything. I advanced with short steps, carefully examining the apartment. Nothing. I inspected every article, one after the other. Still nothing. I went over to the window. The shutters, large wooden shutters, were open. I shut them with great care, and then drew the curtains, enormous velvet curtains, and placed a chair in front of them, so as to have nothing to fear from outside.

Then I cautiously sat down. The armchair was solid. I did not venture to get into the bed. However, the night was advancing; and I ended by coming to the conclusion that I was foolish. If they were spying on me, as I supposed, they must, while waiting for the success of the joke they had been preparing for me, have been laughing immoderately at my terror. So I made up my mind to go to bed. But the bed was particularly suspicious-looking. I pulled at the curtains. They seemed to be secure.

All the same, there was danger. I was going perhaps to receive a cold shower both from overhead, or perhaps, the moment I stretched myself out, to find myself sinking to the floor with my mattress. I searched in my memory for all the practical jokes of which I ever had experience. And I did not want to be caught. Ah! Certainly not! Certainly not! Then I suddenly bethought myself of a precaution which I considered insured safety. I caught hold of the side of the mattress gingerly, and very slowly drew it toward me. It came away, followed by the sheet and the rest of the bedclothes. I dragged all these objects into the very middle of the room, facing the entrance door. I made my bed over again as best I could at some distance from the suspected bedstead and the corner which had filled me with such anxiety. Then I extinguished all the candles, and, groping my way, I slipped under the bed clothes.

For at least another hour I remained awake, starting at the slightest sound. Everything seemed quiet in the chateau. I fell asleep.

I must have been in a deep sleep for a long time, but all of a sudden I was awakened with a start by the fall of a heavy body tumbling right on top of my own, and, at the same time, I received on my face, on my neck, and on my chest a burning liquid which made me utter a howl of pain. And a dreadful noise, as if a sideboard laden with plates and dishes had fallen down, almost deafened me.

I was smothering beneath the weight that was crushing me and preventing me from moving. I stretched out my hand to find out what was the nature of this object. I felt a face, a nose, and whiskers. Then, with all my strength, I launched out a blow at this face. But I immediately received a hail of cuffings which made me jump straight out of the soaked sheets, and rush in my nightshirt into the corridor, the door of which I found open.

Oh, heavens! It was broad daylight. The noise brought my friends hurrying into my apartment, and we found, sprawling over my improvised bed, the dismayed valet, who, while bringing me my morning cup of tea, had tripped over this obstacle in the middle of the floor and fallen on his stomach, spilling my breakfast over my face in spite of himself.

The precautions I had taken in closing the shutters and going to sleep in the middle of the room had only brought about the practical joke I had been trying to avoid.

Oh, how they all laughed that day!

你准备好了吗

这部纪录片讲述了一个富兰克林远征的故事,这次远征是绝望的,注定会失败。它同样讲述了为找出问题所在进行的同样绝望的挣扎。1845 年,约翰·富兰克林爵士带着两艘船和 132 名士兵,出发去寻找一条穿越北极到亚洲的航线——传说中的"西北通道"。他们出发了却再也没有回来。探险失败的原因成为一个永恒的谜。150 年后,富兰克林的记录仍然缺失,对他的船只和士兵坟墓的搜寻仍在继续。

早在 16 世纪,英国就企图征服北极。但是路途艰难——世界第二大冰雪覆盖的岛屿基本上是未知的,"西北通道"是否还存在并不确定。但是,富兰克林决心证明这一切是可以做到的。他的船驶向巴芬湾,最终被发现船停泊在冰川上。直到今天,没人知道接下来发生了什么。真正完成这次探险的是他所用的地图,这些地图是精确记录的细节、空白和猜测的大杂烩。由于公众舆论认为威廉国王岛实际上是大陆的一部分,富兰克林就此得出结论认为该通道向东是封闭的。因此,他向西航行,他的船被困在冰层中。船上的人没有可以求助的资源,只能等待夏天的来临,祈祷在变得越来越厚的冰层穿透船体之前冰消雪融。

安妮·迪拉德在她的《教石头说话》一书中,揭示了一个悲伤而凄美的故事,讲述了当我们准备不足时就贸然出发会产生什么后果。她讲述了一支英国北极探险队的故事,这支探险队于 1845 年启航,绘制了从加拿大北极圈到太平洋的西北航道图。两艘船，以及船上的138名人员均未返回。

约翰·富兰克林爵士船长做了准备，好像他们要踏上快乐的旅程，而不是一场穿越地球上最恶劣环境之一的艰辛旅程。他打包了1200册图书，相当于一个图书馆的藏书量。他为军官和士兵每人准备了一套外观精美、设计烦琐的手工瓷器、玻璃酒杯和纯银餐具。多年以后，在那些冰冷的、支离破碎的尸体旁还能找到这些餐具。

当船驶入寒冷的水域并陷入冰层中时，此次航行注定会失败。首先，甲板被冰层、翼梁和索具所覆盖。然后水在舵周围结冰，船无可救药地困在了已经结冰的海里。

水手们开始寻求帮助，但很快就死于北极严寒的天气、强风和亚冻结低温。在大约20年的时间里，在整个冰冻的土地上发现了远征队队员的遗骸。

船员们既没有为寒冷做好准备，也没有为船只被冰封做任何准备。在历时两到三年的航行中，他们只准备了海军制服，船长只为辅助蒸汽机携带了为期12天的煤炭供应。最后，在离船只数英里的地方发现了船长冰冻的尸体，穿着他那精致的蓝色制服，配以真丝彩色穗带，一件蓝色外套和一条丝绸领巾。这是高贵而受人尊敬的服装，但完全不适当。

历史学家可能会对这种准备不足的旅程所表现出的智慧表示怀疑。但对我们来说更重要的问题是——我们是否也为自己的踏上我们称之为"生命"的漫长旅程做好了准备？我们是否已为前路即将出现的一切做好了准备？

在生理和心理上，我们准备好了去应对可能发生的事情了吗？我们是否定期通过日常学习和锻炼来保持健康？我们的思想和身体是否准备好了应对将要出现的挑战？

我们在情感上和精神上准备好了吗？我们是否践行爱、喜悦、和平、耐心、仁慈、温柔、忠诚、善良和自制等美德？去迎接未知的将来，我们在情感上和精神上准备好了吗？

未做好准备就贸然踏上旅程，可能会给我们带来灾难性的后果。但是好消息是，我们仍然还可以为自己做准备。在很大程度上，我们航行的成功将取决于我们的日常和系统准备。

你准备好了吗？

Are You Ready

This documentary recounts a desperate tale of the doomed Franklin expedition and the equally desperate struggle to find out what went wrong. In 1845, Sir John Franklin, with two ships and 132 men, set out to find a route to Asia through the arctic—the fabled Northwest Passage. They never returned. Why the expedition failed became an enduring mystery. After 150 years, Franklin's records are still missing and the search for his ships and the graves of his men continues.

Since the 16th century, the British had been trying to conquer the Arctic. But the way was hard—the ice-encrusted islands of the world's second largest archipelago were largely uncharted, and it was uncertain if the Northwest Passage even existed. However, Franklin was determined to prove that it could be done. His ships sailed for Baffin Bay, where they were last seen moored to an iceberg. To this day, no one knows what happened next. What really finished the expedition were its maps, which were a mixture of accurately recorded detail, blank spaces and conjecture. Since popular opinion maintained that King William Island was in fact part of the mainland, Franklin concluded that the passage was closed off to the east. He therefore sailed west, where his ships became trapped in the ice. The men onboard had no recourse but to wait for the summer and pray that the ice thawed before it grew thick enough to burst through the hulls.

In her book *Teaching a Stone to Talk*, Annie Dillard reveals a sad, but poignant story about what happens when we set out unprepared. She tells of a British Arctic expedition which set sail in 1845 to chart the Northwest Passage around the Canadian Arctic to the Pacific Ocean. Neither of the two ships and none of the 138 men aboard returned.

Captain Sir John Franklin prepared as if they were embarking on a pleasure cruise rather than an arduous and grueling journey through one of earth's most hostile environments. He packed a 1,200 volume library, a hand-organ, china place settings for officers and men, cut-glass wine goblets and sterling silver flatware, beautifully and intricately designed. Years later, some of these place settings would be found near a clump of frozen, cannibalised bodies.

The voyage was doomed when the ships sailed into frigid waters and became trapped in ice. First ice coated the decks, the spars and the rigging. Then water froze around the rudders and the ships became hopelessly locked in the now-frozen sea.

Sailors set out to search for help, but soon succumbed to

severe Arctic weather and died of exposure to its harsh winds and sub-freezing temperatures. For some twenty years, remains of the expeditions were found all over the frozen landscape.

The crew did not prepare either for the cold or for the eventuality of the ships becoming ice-locked. On a voyage which was to last two to three years, they packed only their Navy-issue uniforms and the captain carried just a 12-day supply of coal for the auxiliary steam engines. The frozen body of an officer was eventually found, miles from the vessel, wearing his uniform of fine blue cloth, edged with silk braid, a blue greatcoat and a silk neckerchief—clothing which was noble and respectful, but wholly inadequate.

Historians may doubt the wisdom of such an ill-prepared journey. But more important for us is the question—Are we, too, prepared for the lengthy voyage we've embarked upon, that journey we call "life"? Have we made ourselves ready for all that will surely await us?

Physically and mentally, are we prepared to handle what may come? Do we regularly stay fit through daily study and exercise? Will our minds and bodies be ready to cope with challenges which will arise?

Emotionally and spiritually, are we ready? Do we practice such virtues as love, joy, peace, patience, kindness, gentleness, faithfulness, goodness and self-control? Will we be emotionally and spiritually ready to embrace an unknown future?

    To embark on a journey unprepared can set us up for disastrous results. But the good news is, we can still prepare for ours. And in large part, the success of our voyage will be determined by our regular and systematic preparation.

    Are you ready?

加里·阿伯特的妈妈

[美国] 戴维·吉普森

"加里,我是妈妈,收到短信速回电话。"

我不知道这个加里是谁,为什么他妈妈要找他,却给我的手机发短信。第二天我在家时,这个女人又打来了电话。

"加里·阿伯特,为什么不给我回电话?"

"我不是加里·阿伯特呀!"我告诉她。"您拨错电话号码了。"

"胡说,"她说,"我能听出你的声音。我打电话是想说你父亲心脏病又犯了。他正躺在波士顿的一家医院里,一直吵着要想见你。"

"但我真的不是加里·阿伯特啊!甚至都不认识叫加里·阿伯特的人!"

"你现在听我说,"她说,"你得去一趟波士顿,我知道你和你爸爸都不喜欢对方,但他毕竟是你爸呀!在这个可怜人死之前,你要内心安宁。这可能是最后一次机会了。"

这个疯狂的女人一口气说了整整二十分钟,事无巨细地说了我(也就是她以为的加里·阿伯特)过去做过每件错事。听了她的话,我还真有点愧疚了。

"好的,我听到了,妈妈。我明白了。"最终我说需要收拾东西前往波士顿，才让她挂了电话。

病房里挤满了闪烁的机器，发出不吉利的声音。这些机器的光很暗淡，一个瘦骨嶙峋的男人躺在床上，皮肤呈蓝灰色。"我来了，爸爸，"我说，"是我，加里！"

他睁开眼睛，慢慢转过头来面向我。沉默了好长时间以后，他终于开口说："你不是我儿子，你看起来一点也不像他。"

"这里光线很暗，"我说，"而且，已经过了那么久。"

"是啊，已经过了那么久了。"他重复着我的话。"现在告诉我，你为什么出现在这里。"

"妈妈说您病得很重，想要见我。"

"胡扯！我是病了，我是因为这个女人和她撒的谎病的。多年以前我就该跟她离婚了，我也没说过要见你。就算我说了，我想你也不会来。"他每说一句话，好像都用尽了全身力气，所以只好停一下喘口气。"那好吧，既然过来了，就说说你现在过得怎么样？"

"我已经改邪归正了，过去四年来重新做人，读完了法学院，正准备参加下个月的律师资格考试。"

"啊，律师？我就知道你不学好。"他闭上眼睛，转过脸去面朝墙。

"爸爸，我是来说抱歉的。"

"抱歉？你到底为什么抱歉？"

"为所有一切，过去所发生的一切，为我所做过的每一件事，我都感到抱歉。我为我不能陪着你感到抱歉，我为我不能再努力点抱歉，我为我让你失望而抱歉。"我很惊讶自己竟然说出这些话来，听起来那么真诚，连我自己都信以为真。我觉得自己快要哭出来了。泪腺打开了，我的眼泪止都止不住地落下来，这是我八九岁以来的第一次。

这个病床上像稻草人似的老人却无动于衷。"永远不要说抱歉，"他说,"即便你真的觉得抱歉。出去吧,让我一个人安静一会儿,还有无论怎样,也不要告诉你妈妈你来过这里。"

第二天我回到家,电话上有一条新留言。"加里,我是妈妈,我打电话是想告诉你,你父亲晚上过世了。我希望你好自为之吧,为什么这一次就不能按我说的做呢,哪怕就一次?我对你失望透顶,别再指望我打电话给你了!"

Gary Abbott's Mother

By David Jibson

"Gary, it's Mother. Call me back as soon as you get this message."

I had no idea who this Gary was, or why his mother would be calling him on my phone. The next day I was home when the same woman called.

"Gary Abbott, why didn't you call me back?"

"I'm not Gary Abbott," I told her. "You have the wrong number."

"Nonsense," she said. "I recognize your voice. I called to tell you that your father's had another heart attack. He's in a hospital in Boston and he's been asking for you."

"But, really, I'm not Gary Abbott. I don't even know a Gary Abbott."

"Now you listen to me," she said. "You get yourself to Boston. I know how much you hate each other, but he's your father and this is probably your last chance to make your peace before the poor man dies."

This crazy woman went for a good twenty minutes, detailing everything I (or rather, Gary Abbott) had ever done wrong. I actually started to feel guilty.

"Yes, okay. I get it, Mother. I understand." I finally convinced her to hang up the phone by telling her that I needed to pack for the trip to Boston.

The room was crowded with blinking machines that made ominous sounds. The lights were dimmed. A scrawny man with blue-gray skin lay in the bed. "I'm here, Pop," I said. "It's me. Gary."

His eyes opened and he slowly turned to face me. After an eternity, he finally said, "You're not my son. You don't look anything like him."

"It's pretty dark in here," I told him. "Besides, it's been a long time."

"Yes, it's been a long time," he repeated back to me. "Now tell me why the hell you're here."

"Mom said you're real sick and you've been asking for me."

"Bullshit! I'm sick alright, sick of that woman and her lies. I should have divorced her years ago. I didn't ask for you. I wouldn't expect you to come if I did." Talking seemed to take all his effort and he had to stop to catch his breath. "Well, as long as you're here, what have you been up to?"

"I've cleaned myself up, been straight going on four years. I finished law school. I'm taking the bar exam next month."

"Lawyer, eh? I always knew you'd come to no good." His eyes closed and he turned his face to the wall.

"Pop, I came here to tell you I'm sorry."

"You're sorry? What the hell are you sorry for?"

"Everything. I'm sorry for everything that's happened, everything I've done. I'm sorry I haven't been around, sorry I didn't try harder, sorry I was such a disappointment." The words coming out of me took me by surprise. They sounded sincere and I think they were. I could feel tears welling inside me. For the first time since I was eight or nine years old, the waterworks started and I could do nothing to stop them.

The old scarecrow in the bed was unmoved. "Never say you're sorry," he said, "even when you mean it. Now get out of here and leave me alone—and whatever you do, don't tell your mother you were here."

When I got home the next day, there was a new message. "Gary, it's Mother. I called to tell you your father died in the night. I hope you're proud of yourself. Why couldn't you do as I asked just this one time? I'm through with you. Don't ever expect me to call again."

流浪猫"丑丑"

我所住公寓大楼的每个人都认识"丑丑"。"丑丑"是住在这里的一只流浪公猫。浮世三千,"丑丑"最爱有三:打架、吃垃圾,还有爱(如果我们可以这样说的话)。

这三点,再加上流浪在外的生活方式,对"丑丑"产生了很大的影响。首先,他只有一只眼睛,另一只只剩下一个洞,同一侧的耳朵也缺了一只。他的左脚显然也曾经严重骨折过,而且没有复原,走起路来一瘸一拐的,好像总在转弯。

"丑丑"原本应该是一只身上带有条纹的深灰色虎斑猫,但他的头部、颈部,甚至肩膀上到处都是伤口。每当有人看到"丑丑"时,他们的反应都是一样的:"这只猫可真丑啊!"

当他试图进入某家某户时,大人都会警告孩子们不要去碰他,大人会向他投掷石块,用水管喷水驱赶他。当他不肯离开时,人们还会关上门夹他的爪子。可面对这些,"丑丑"的反应总是一样的。

当你将水管对准他时,他会站在那里一动不动,任由你把他全身淋湿,直到你放弃并离开。当你向他投掷东西时,他会将自己瘦长的身体蜷缩在你的脚边,告诉你他原谅了你。

每当他看到孩子们时,都会跑过去,疯狂地喵喵叫,用头碰撞孩子们的手,乞求他们的爱。

当你抱起他时,他就会马上开始舔你的衬衫、耳环,还有他能从你身上找到的所有东西。

有一天,"丑丑"向邻居家的几条狗表达爱意,但他们并没有做出善意的回应,"丑丑"受到了粗暴的对待,伤势严重。我试图冲上去帮他。但当我到达他倒下的地方时,看上去"丑丑"的悲惨一生已快走到了尽头。

我把他抱起来,试图把他带回家。此时,我可以听到他吃力的喘息声,同时能够感觉到他在挣扎。我想,这一定给他的身心造成了重创。

接下来,我感觉到耳朵有一种熟悉的、被拉扯的感觉。"丑丑"在这样极度痛苦的时候,显而易见在承受着濒临死亡痛苦的时候,可还是在努力地舔着我的耳朵。我抱他抱得更紧了,他用头碰撞着我的手掌,然后他那只金色的眼睛转过来望着我。此时,我可以清晰地听到他发出的呼噜声。

即使在最痛苦的时候,这只被咬得伤痕累累的猫还在渴望一点点爱抚,或许只是一些同情。那一刻,我觉得"丑丑"是我见过的最美丽、最可爱的动物。他从来没有试图咬我或抓我,从来没有试图远离我,也从来没有以任何方式挣脱我的怀抱。"丑丑"只是抬头望着我,完全相信我能够缓解他的痛苦。

我还没来得及走进家门,"丑丑"就已经死在了我的怀里。之后,我抱着他坐了很久,心里思考着——这样一只满身伤痕而且身体还有残缺的小流浪猫,是如何改变了我对拥有一颗纯真心灵,以及全心全意、真心实意去爱的看法。

关于给予与同情,我从"丑丑"身上学到了很多东西,比读成千上万本书籍、听成千上万次讲座、看成千上万次脱口秀特别节目都要多得多。为此，我会永远心存感激。他的伤痕在身上，我的伤痕在心里。是时候啦，我要继续前行，学会全心全意、掏心掏肺地去爱，为我在乎的人付出我的所有。

许多人希望变得更富有、更成功、更受欢迎、更美丽，而我不是，我永远都希望变成"丑丑"。

Ugly the Cat

Everyone in the apartment complex I lived in knew who Ugly was. Ugly was the resident tomcat. Ugly loved three things in this world: fighting, eating garbage, and, shall we say, love.

The combination of these things combined with a life spent outside had their effect on Ugly. To start with, he had only one eye and where the other should have been was a hole. He was also missing his ear on the same side, his left foot appeared to have been badly broken at one time, and had healed at an unnatural angle, making him look like he was always turning the corner.

Ugly would have been a dark grey tabby, striped type, except for the sores covering his head, neck, and even his shoulders. Every time someone saw Ugly there was the same reaction: "That's one UGLY cat!"

All the children were warned not to touch him, the adults threw rocks at him, hosed him down, squirted him when he tried to come in their homes, or shut his paws in the door when he would not leave. Ugly always had the same reaction.

If you turned the hose on him, he would stand there, getting soaked until you gave up and quit. If you threw things at him, he would curl his lanky body around your feet in forgiveness.

Whenever he spied children, he would come running, meowing frantically and bump his head against their hands, begging for their love.

If you ever picked him up he would immediately begin suckling on your shirt, earrings, whatever he could find.

One day Ugly shared his love with the neighbours' dogs. They did not respond kindly, and Ugly was badly mauled. I tried to rush to his aid. By the time I got to where he was laying, it was apparent Ugly's sad life was almost at an end.

As I picked him up and tried to carry him home, I could hear him wheezing and gasping, and could feel him struggling. It must be hurting him terribly, I thought.

Then I felt a familiar tugging, sucking sensation on my ear. Ugly, in so much pain, suffering and obviously dying, was trying to suckle my ear. I pulled him closer to me, and he bumped the palm of my hand with his head, then he turned his one golden eye towards me, and I could hear the distinct sound of purring.

Even in the greatest pain, that ugly battled scarred cat was asking only for a little affection, perhaps some compassion. At that moment I thought Ugly was the most beautiful, loving creature I had ever seen. Never once did he try to bite or scratch me, try to get away from me, or struggle in any way. Ugly just looked up at me completely trusting in me to relieve his pain.

Ugly died in my arms before I could get inside, but I sat and held him for a long time afterwards, thinking about how one scarred, deformed little stray could so alter my opinion about what it means to have true pureness of spirit, to love so totally and truly.

Ugly taught me more about giving and compassion than a thousand books, lectures, or talk show specials ever could, and for that I will always be thankful. He had been scarred on the outside, but I was scarred on the inside, and it was time for me to move on and learn to love truly and deeply. To give my total to those I cared for.

Many people want to be richer, more successful, well liked, beautiful, but for me; I will always try to be Ugly.

鬼 屋

[英国] 弗吉尼亚·伍尔芙

无论什么时候醒来,总能听到关门的声音。他们手牵着手,从一个房间走到另一个房间,揭开这个看看,打开那里看看,一一确认——他们是一对鬼夫妻。

"我们把它放在了这里。"她说。"哦,还有这里!"他补充道。"在楼上。"她喃喃细语。"还有花园里。"他耳语道。"小点声,"他们异口同声,"不然会吵醒他们的。"

吵醒我们的不是你们。哦,不是的。"找它的是他们;拉上窗帘的是他们。"有人可能这样推测,然后继续读上一两页书。"现在他们找到它了。"有人确认,手中的铅笔停在页边空白处。后来书读累了,有人站起来走过去亲自看看;房子里空荡荡的,所有的门都开着,只有斑鸠发出心满意足的咕咕声,以及从农场传来打谷机的隆隆声。"我来这里做什么?想找什么?"我两手空空。"它或许上楼了吧?"阁楼里存放着苹果。于是下了楼,花园依然静悄悄的,书却滑落在草地上。

他们已经在客厅找到它了。其实那个它永远不可能看见他们。窗户的玻璃上映出了苹果树,也映出了蔷薇;叶子都是绿油油的。如果他们在客厅里走动,苹果只转过了黄色的那一面。而片刻过后,如果门开了,影子便投在地上,搭在墙上,挂在天花板上——什么?我两手空空。一只画眉的投影掠过地毯,斑鸠的咕咕声仿佛来自寂静的森林幽深的井里。"很安全,很安全,很安全。"房子的脉搏轻轻地跳动着。"珍宝埋起来了;房间……"脉搏突然停止了跳动。啊,那就是埋藏的珍宝吗?

不一会儿,灯光暗了下来。那么,走出(房子)进入花园了吗?那里树影婆娑,为了一缕漂泊的阳光。多么美好,多么难得啊,那些我曾经一直在玻璃窗后面追逐的、燃烧的光线,现在冷漠地沉入光线下。玻璃即死亡,我们之间隔着死亡。几百年前,先是来到女人面前,离开房子,封了所有的窗户;那些房间从此不见光亮。他离开了房子,离开了女人,去过北边,去过东边,也看过南边天空上变幻的星星。寻找房子,发现它坐落在山脚下。"很安全,很安全,很安全。"房子的脉搏高兴地跳动着。"珍宝是你们的。"

风沿着林荫道呼啸而来。树随之前仰后合。月光在雨中肆意地迸溅流溢。可是,灯光却从窗户中直射出来。蜡烛僵直地燃烧着。这对鬼夫妻在房子里漫步穿行,打开一扇扇窗户,追寻欢乐,轻言细语生怕吵醒我们。

"我们在这里睡过。"她说。他补充道:"吻过无数次。"

"早晨醒来——""林间银光闪烁——"

"在楼上——""在花园里——""夏天来临的时候——"

"冬天下雪的时候——"远处的门一个一个地关上了,叩击声轻得仿佛心脏的跳动。

他们越来越近,最后停在了门口。风小了,雨水闪烁着银光,从玻璃窗上滑落。我们眼前漆黑一片,听不见身边的脚步声,也看不见披着披风、裙袂飘飘的女鬼。他用手将提灯遮住。"看,"他轻声说道,

"睡得多香。他们的唇上还有爱意。"

他们提着银质罩灯,弯下腰久久凝视着我们。这样子过了很久,一阵风直直地吹来,火焰轻轻摇曳。月光洒满地板,和墙壁相遇,给他们的脸染上了颜色。他们的面孔做沉思状,他们的面孔寻找这睡觉的人,也寻找着深藏在他们心底的快乐。

"很安全,很安全,很安全。"房子的心脏自豪地跳动着。

"这么多年——"他叹息道,"你又找到了我。""我们,"她低声说道,"在这里睡觉;在花园里读书;在阁楼上滚苹果,欢声笑语。我们在这里留下了我们的珍宝——"他们俯下身子,他们银质罩灯的光闪得我睁开了眼睛。"很安全!很安全!很安全!"房子的脉搏狂跳不已。我醒了过来,喊道:"啊,这就是你们埋藏的珍宝吗?心中的光。"

A Haunted House

By Virginia Woolf

Whatever hour you woke there was a door shutting. From room to room they went, hand in hand, lifting here, opening there, making sure—a ghostly couple.

"Here we left it," she said. And he added, "Oh, but here too!" "It's upstairs," she murmured. "And in the garden," he whispered. "Quietly," they said, "or we shall wake them."

But it wasn't that you woke us. Oh, no. "They're looking for it; they're drawing the curtain," one might say, and so read on a page or two. "Now they've found it," one would be certain, stopping the pencil on the margin. And then, tired of reading, one might rise and see for oneself, the house all empty, the doors standing open, only the wood pigeons bubbling with content and the hum of the threshing machine sounding from the farm. "What did I come in here for? What did I want to find?" My hands were empty. "Perhaps it's upstairs then?" The apples were in the loft. And so down again, the garden still as ever, only the book had slipped into the grass.

But they had found it in the drawing room. Not that one could ever see them. The window panes reflected apples, reflected roses; all the leaves were green in the glass. If they moved in the drawing room, the apple only turned its yellow side. Yet, the moment after, if the door was opened, spread about the floor, hung upon the walls, pendant from the ceiling—what? My hands were empty. The shadow of a thrush crossed the carpet; from the deepest wells of silence the wood pigeon drew its bubble of sound. "Safe, safe, safe," the pulse of the house beat softly. "The treasure buried; the room…" the pulse stopped short. Oh, was that the buried treasure?

A moment later the light had faded. Out in the garden then? But the trees spun darkness for a wandering beam of sun. So fine, so rare, coolly sunk beneath the surface the beam I sought always burnt behind the glass. Death was the glass; death was between us; coming to the woman first, hundreds of years ago, leaving the house, sealing all the windows; the rooms were darkened. He left it, left her, went North, went East, saw the stars turned in the Southern sky; sought the house, found it dropped beneath the Downs. "Safe, safe, safe," the pulse of the house beat gladly. "The Treasure yours."

The wind roars up the avenue. Trees stoop and bend this way and that. Moonbeams splash and spill wildly in the rain. But the beam of the lamp falls straight from the window. The candle burns stiff and still. Wandering through the house, opening the windows, whispering not to wake us, the ghostly couple seek their joy.

"Here we slept," she says. And he adds, "Kisses without number."

"Waking in the morning—" "Silver between the trees—"

"Upstairs—" "In the garden—" "When summer came—"

"In winter snow time—" The doors go shutting far in the distance, gently knocking like the pulse of a heart.

Nearer they come; cease at the doorway. The wind falls, the rain slides silver down the glass. Our eyes darken; we hear no steps beside us; we see no lady spread her ghostly cloak. His hands shield the lantern. "Look," he breathes. "Sound asleep. Love upon their lips."

Stooping, holding their silver lamp above us, long they look and deeply. Long they pause. The wind drives straightly; the flame stoops slightly. Wild beams of moonlight cross both floor and wall, and, meeting, stain the faces bent; the faces pondering; the faces that search the sleepers and seek their hidden joy.

"Safe, safe, safe," the heart of the house beats proudly.

"Long years—" he sighs. "Again you found me." "Here," she murmurs, "sleeping; in the garden reading; laughing, rolling apples in the loft. Here we left our treasure—" Stooping, their light lifts the lids upon my eyes. "Safe! safe! safe!" the pulse of the house beats wildly. Waking, I cry "Oh, is this your buried treasure? The light in the heart."

天使的伪装

[美国] 蒂莫西·谢伊·亚瑟

死去的母亲冷冰冰地、一动不动地躺在那里，她可怜的孩子们就围在她身边。这个女人活着时，几乎被村里的男女老少所有人鄙视。几位邻居匆匆忙忙来到她那破旧不堪、摇摇欲坠的小屋子里，在那里曾在半饥半饱的情况下养活了她的三个孩子。

三个孩子里年龄最长的是约翰，一个身体壮实的12岁大男孩，已经能够与其他农夫一起干活谋生。10岁多一点、11岁还不到的凯特是一个聪明伶俐、性格活泼的小女孩，她的脑子里总是会蹦出许多鬼点子。但年龄最小的、可怜的小玛吉，却患上了不治之症。两年前，她从窗户摔下来伤到了脊椎，从那以后她再也没下过床。所以没有一个人说"我来收养玛吉"，而凯特和约翰很快就被善良且没儿没女的夫妇收养照顾了。说到底，谁会想要一个卧床不起的孩子呢？

"把她送救济院吧。"一个粗鲁的男人说。"对于这个乳臭未干的小孩儿，这肯定是个幸运的改变，在那里，她会有干净的环境，吃上健康的食物，生病了有医生给她看病，可以说这比她过去的状况好多了。"此时，一位名叫乔·汤普森的车匠碰巧从这里经过。他停下脚步，对那个男人说："把她送到那种地方太残忍了。""啊，汤普森先生！"玛吉哀求道,"不要把我一个人留在这里!"

看起来是个粗人的乔·汤普森先生其实是个有爱心的人,有时候还特别温柔。他喜欢孩子,很乐意他们来他的店里。"不,亲爱的,"他回答说,"我不会把你一个人留在这里的。"他用自己强壮的臂膀抱起她,走到门外,穿过田地回到了他的家。

"你手里抱着什么?"汤普森太太急促地质问刚刚回到家的汤普森先生。"等一会儿再跟你解释,先别急。"乔用同样急促的语气回答。他把玛吉抱到一楼的一个小房间里,放在床上。然后,他走出房间,关上门,与他那尖酸刻薄的妻子面对面。

"你该不是把那病恹恹的孩子带回家了吧!?"她怒气冲冲地问道。"我觉得女人的心肠有时候很硬。"乔说。他通常会避开冷冰冰的妻子,或者在她火冒三丈的时候一声不吭,不跟她一般见识。"女人的心没男人的一半硬!"她说。乔看出自己突然一反常态,这种坚决态度使妻子意识到了事情的严重性,于是迅速回答道:"农夫琼斯把她的哥哥约翰扔进他的马车里,然后开车离开了。她的姐姐凯特和埃利斯太太一起回家了。但是,没人想要这个可怜的病孩子。'把她送到救济院去'成了最后的结论。""那你把她带回来干什么?"他的妻子不耐烦地说道。"她没法自己走去救济院,"乔回答说,"必须有人伸出臂膀把她抱过去,而我臂膀非常有劲,有能力完成这项任务。"

"那你为什么要在家里停留?"妻子追问道。"因为把她送去之前,必须先见到救济院的管理员,并取得入院许可。""你什么时候去见管理员?"她不耐烦地问道。"明天。""为什么要等到明天?""简,"车匠用一种感人的口吻对他妻子说,这种口吻把他妻子镇住了,"对于我们来说,把这个可怜的、失去母亲的小家伙留一个晚上只是小事一桩。只善待她一个晚上,让她在这里舒舒服服地待一个晚上。"

这个强壮、粗糙的男人的声音开始颤抖,然后他将头转向了另一侧,好掩饰他湿润的眼睛。汤普森太太什么也没说,但一种温柔的感觉潜入了她的内心。"亲切地看着她,简,然后亲切地跟她说话,"乔说,"想想她死去的母亲,还有她在即将到来的生活中不得不面对的孤独、痛苦和悲伤。"汤普森太太仍然一言不发,却转向她丈夫暂时安置玛吉的那个小房间,推开门,安静地走了进去。乔没有跟进去,他觉得最好让她独自和那孩子待一会儿。于是,他去了自己的店铺,一直工作到傍晚才回家。家里那个小房间的窗户透出微弱的灯光,唤起了乔赶快回到家里的渴望:这是个好兆头。

他忍不住透过小房间的窗户向里看,只见玛吉正聚精会神地凝视着他的妻子。他妻子脸上的表情悲伤而温柔,没有了平素的冷漠、怨恨或痛苦。进了家门,乔没有随即去小房间。他的妻子却有点匆忙地从那个小房间出来迎接他。"晚饭还要多长时间能做好?"他问。"马上就好。"汤普森太太答道,那口吻里有伪装的冷漠,然后就忙开了。

乔坐在餐桌前等待他的妻子来挑明在他俩心中最重要的话题,时间一分一秒地过去,她还是只字未提。最后,她突然开了口:"你打算怎么处置那个孩子?""我觉得你已经理解了我的意思,就是送她去救济院。"乔回答说,装出对她的问题很惊讶的样子。汤普森太太用非常奇怪的眼神看着她的丈夫,然后垂下了眼睛。晚餐时,没有人再提及这个话题。他们吃完饭后,汤普森太太烤了一片面包,然后用牛奶和黄油把它泡软了,又沏上一杯茶。她把这些一起带进了玛吉的房间。饥肠辘辘的孩子一边吃着,一边用各种可能的方式表达着内心的快乐,并向汤普森太太投去了感激的目光,这眼神唤醒了她内心深处原始的人类情感。

"我们可以留她多住一两天,她太虚弱,太需要帮助了。"汤普森太太在第二天吃早餐时对她丈夫前一天的话做出了这样的回答。"她对你的生活影响会很大的,"乔说道,"对于我来说,不会介意她多住一两天的,可怜的孩子!"事实上,还不到一个星期,汤普森太太已经把将玛吉送到救济院的念头丢到了脑后。她把孩子抱在怀里,同时也放进了她的心里,孩子便成了一个宝贵的负担。对于乔·汤普森先生来说,这个孩子的到来,就像家里住进了一位天使,让他沉闷的家充满了爱的阳光,只不过这位天使伪装成一个生病、无助、悲惨的孩子的样子。

An Angel in Disguise

By Timothy Shay Arthur

The dead mother lay cold and still amid her wretched children. This woman had been despised by nearly every man, woman, and child in the village. Neighbours went hastily to her old tumble-down hut, in which she had secured her half-starving children, three in number.

Of these, John, the oldest, a boy of twelve, was a stout lad, able to earn his living with any farmer. Kate, between ten and eleven, was a bright, active girl, out of whom something clever might be made; but poor little Maggie, the youngest, was hopelessly diseased. Two years before, a fall from a window had injured her spine, and she had not been able to leave her bed since. So no one said: "I'll take Maggie", while Kate and John quickly were taken care of by kind, childless couples. After all, who wanted a bed-ridden child?

"Take her to the poorhouse," said a rough man. "For this brat it will prove a blessed change, she will be kept clean, have healthy food, and be doctored, which is more than can be said of her past condition." Joe Thompson, a wheelwright who happened to pass by, paused, and said to him: "It's a cruel thing to put her there." "O, Mr. Thompson!" Maggie cried out, "Don't leave me here all alone!"

Though rough in exterior, Joe Thompson had a heart, and it was very tender in some places. He liked children, and was pleased to have them come to his shop. "No, dear," he answered, "You shall not be left alone." Lifting her in his strong arms, he bore her out into the air and across the field to his home.

"What have you there?" sharply questioned Mrs. Thompson upon his return home. "Wait a moment for explanations, and be gentle." Joe said equally sharply back. He carried Maggie to a small chamber on the first floor, and laid her on a bed. Then, stepping back, he shut the door, and stood face to face with his vinegar-tempered wife.

"You haven't brought home that sick brat!" Her face was in a flame. "I think women's hearts are sometimes very hard," said Joe. Usually he got out of his cold wife's way, or kept silent and non-combative when she fired up. "Women's hearts are not half so hard as men's!" She said. Joe saw that his sudden resoluteness had impressed his wife and he answered quickly: "Farmer Jones tossed her brother John into his wagon, and drove off. Her sister Kate went home with Mrs. Ellis; but nobody wanted the poor sick one. 'Send her to the poorhouse,' was the concluding cry." "What did you bring her here for then?" his wife snapped. "She can't walk to the poorhouse," said Joe, "somebody's arms must carry her, and mine are strong enough for that task."

"Then why did you stop here?" demanded the wife. "Because the poorhouse's Guardians must first be seen, and a permit obtained." "When will you see the Guardians?" She asked impatiently. "Tomorrow." "Why put it off till tomorrow?" "Jane," said the wheelwright, with an impressiveness of tone that greatly subdued his wife, "It is a small thing for us to keep this poor motherless little one for a single night; to be kind to her for a single night; to make her life comfortable for a single night."

The voice of the strong, rough man shook, and he turned his head away, so that the moisture in his eyes could not be seen. Mrs. Thompson did not answer, but a soft feeling crept into her heart. "Look at her kindly, Jane; speak to her kindly," said Joe. "Think of her dead mother, and the loneliness, the pain, the sorrow that must be on all her coming life." Mrs. Thompson did not reply, but turned towards the little chamber where her husband had deposited Maggie; and, pushing open the door, went quietly in. Joe did not follow; he felt that it would be best to leave her alone with the child. So he went to his shop, and worked until the evening released him from labour. A light shining through the little chamber window was the first thing that made Joe eager to return to the house: it was a good omen.

He could not help looking in through the little chamber window. Maggie's eyes were intently fixed upon his wife; her expression was sad and tender; but he saw nothing of her usual coldness, bitterness or pain. On entering, Joe did not go immediately to the little chamber. His wife somewhat hurriedly came to him from the room where she had been with Maggie. "How soon will supper be ready?" he asked. "Right soon," answered Mrs. Thompson in a feigned, cold tone while she began to bustle about.

Joe waited, after sitting down to the table, for his wife to introduce the subject uppermost in both of their thoughts; but she kept silent on that theme, for many minutes. At last she said, abruptly; "What are you going to do with that child?" "I thought you understood me that she was to go to the poorhouse," replied Joe, as if surprised at her question. Mrs. Thompson looked rather strangely at her husband, and then lowered her eyes. The subject was not again referred to during the meal. After they finished Mrs. Thompson toasted a slice of bread and softened it with milk and butter. Adding to this a cup of tea, she took this into Maggie's room. The hungry child ate with every sign of pleasure possible and gave Mrs. Thompson a look of gratitude that awoke old human feelings which had been slumbering in her heart for years.

"We'll keep her a day or two longer; she is so weak and helpless," said Mrs. Thompson, in answer to her husband's remark, at breakfast time on the next morning. "She'll be so much in your way," said Joe. "I shan't mind that for a day or two. Poor thing!" In fact, in less than a week Mrs. Thompson would leave all thought of sending Maggie to the poorhouse. She carried her in her heart as well as in her arms; a precious burden. As for Joe Thompson, an angel had come into his house, disguised as a sick, helpless, and miserable child, and filled all its dreary chambers with the sunshine of love.

我的导师

当伟大的苏菲派潜修者哈桑在弥留之际,有人问道:"哈桑,你的导师是谁?"

他回答道:"我有成千上万的导师,哪怕我仅仅简单提一下他们的名字,也需要几个月、几年时间,时间不够了,但是,其中三位我一定要告诉你。"

我的第一位导师是一个贼。有一次,我在荒漠中迷了路,当我最终到达了一个村庄的时候,天色已经太晚了,家家户户都房门紧闭。最后我发现一个人正在一座房子的墙上挖洞,我问他,我能待在什么地方?他回答说,深更半夜的,比较困难,如果你愿意和一个贼待在一起的话,那你就和我待在一起得了。

其实,这个人长得挺漂亮的,我跟他在一起待了一个月呢!每到夜里,他都会对我说:"我要出去工作了,你休息,祈祷吧。"当他回来时,我问他:"你今天有收获吗?"他总是会说:"今晚没有,但是,按照安拉的旨意,明天就会好起来的。"他从来都不会绝望过,总是快快乐乐的。

我一连苦思冥想了许多年,没有任何事情发生。我总是想到这个贼,很多次,当我极度绝望的时候,我想不要再胡闹了。我会突然想起那个贼,想起每个晚上他都会说的那句话:"按照安拉的旨意,明天就会好起来的。"

我的第二位导师是一条狗。我因口渴来到一条河边,这时,一条狗也来了。它也渴了,它向河里望了望,它看到了另外一条狗——它的影子,它很害怕,叫了两声,转身逃走了。但是,因为极度的口渴,它又回来了。最后,尽管恐惧,它还是跳进了河里,河中的影子马上消失了。借此我得到了一条来自安拉的信息:虽然那么恐惧,还是要跳进河里。

我的第三位导师是一个小男孩。我在城里,碰到一个小男孩,手里拿着一支点着的蜡烛,他正准备到清真寺去,把蜡烛放在那里。

"开个玩笑,"我对小男孩说,"是你自己点亮的这支蜡烛吗?"他回答道:"是的,先生。"我又问道:"这蜡烛有亮的时候,有不亮的时候,你能告诉我,这光亮来自哪里吗?"

小男孩哈哈大笑,"噗"的一声吹灭了蜡烛,问道:"你亲眼看到这束光刚刚离去了,你能告诉我它去哪里了吗?"

我的自负一下子破灭了。我的所有知识破灭了。那一瞬间,我彻底感到了自己的愚蠢。从那时候起,我再也不以博学自居了。

事实上,我没有导师,我没有导师并不意味着我不是弟子……我把世间存在的万事万物都视为我的导师,我的门徒生涯比你的更广阔。我信任白云,树木。我信任这样的存在。我没有导师是因为我有千千万万个导师,来源五花八门。做一个门徒就是在路上。做一个门徒意味着什么?意味着学习的能力,意味着准备向脆弱的存在学习。有了一个导师以后,你就开始学习如何学习了。

导师是一个游泳池,你在游泳池里学游泳。一旦你学会了游泳,所有的海洋都会属于你的。

My Masters

When the great Sufi mystic, Hasan, was dying, somebody asked "Hasan, who was your master?"

He said, "I had thousands of masters. If I just relate their names it will take months, years and it is too late. But three masters I will certainly tell you about."

One was a thief. Once I got lost in the desert, and when I reached a village it was very late, everything was closed. But at last I found one man who was trying to make a hole in the wall of a house. I asked him where I could stay and he said: "At this time of night it will be difficult, but you can say with me—if you can stay with a thief."

And the man was so beautiful. I stayed for one month! And each night he would say to me, "Now I am going to my work. You rest, you pray." When he came back I would ask "Could you get anything?" He would say, "Not tonight. But tomorrow I will try again, God willing." He was never in a state of hopelessness, he was always happy.

When I was meditating and meditating for years on end and

nothing was happening, many times the moment came when I was so desperate, so hopeless, that I thought to stop all this nonsense. And suddenly I would remember the thief who would say every night, "God willing, tomorrow it is going to happen."

And my second master was a dog. I was going to the river, thirsty and a dog came. He was also thirsty. He looked into the river, he saw another dog there—his own image—and became afraid. He would bard and run away, but his thirst was so much that he would come back. Finally, despite his fear, he just jumped into the water, and the image disappeared. And I knew that a message had come to me from God: one has to jump in spite of all fears.

And the third master was a small child. I entered a town and a child was carrying a lit candle. he was going to the mosque to put the candle there.

"Just joking," I asked the boy, "Have you lit the candle yourself?" He said, "Yes sir." And I asked, "There was a moment when the candle was unlit, then there was a moment when the candle was lit. Can you show me the source from which the light came?"

And the boy laughed, blew out the candle, and said, "Now you have seen the light going. Where has it gone? You will tell me!"

My ego was shattered, my whole knowledge was shattered. And that moment I felt my own stupidity. Since then I dropped all my knowledgeability.

It is true that I had no master. That does not mean that I was not a disciple—I accepted the whole existence as my master. My Disciplehood was a greater involvement than yours is. I trusted the clouds, the trees. I trusted existence as such. I had no master because I had millions of masters I learned from every possible source. To be a disciple is a must on the path. What does it mean to be a disciple? It means to be able to learn. to be available to learn to be vulnerable to existence. With a master you start learning to learn.

The master is a swimming pool where you can learn how to swim. Once you have learned, all the oceans are yours.

石 匠

[美国] 詹姆斯·鲍德温

好多好多年以前,意大利住着一个名叫安东尼奥·卡诺瓦的小男孩。他的父亲去世了,于是他与爷爷住在一起。爷爷是个石匠,一个一贫如洗的石匠。

安东尼奥是个瘦小羸弱的男孩子,身体不够强壮,无法出去工作。他不愿意与小镇里的孩子们一起玩耍,却喜欢跟着爷爷一起去石场。老人忙着切割修整大石头时,小男孩就在小碎石堆里自己玩。有时他会做个软黏土小雕像,有时也会拿起锤子和凿子,试着从大石块上凿下一小块石头。他展现出的纯熟技巧让爷爷大喜过望。

"这孩子将来会成为一位雕塑家。"他说。

然后,他们晚上收工回到家,奶奶总会这样说:"我的小雕塑家,你今天又有了什么作品呀?"

奶奶会把他抱在膝上,唱歌给他听,或给他讲故事,这些故事非常有画面感,让他的脑海里充满了美丽而奇妙的东西。第二天当他回到石场时,他就会试着把那些美好的事物都呈现在石块或黏土块上。

这个小镇上还住着一位叫伯爵的有钱人,有时伯爵会吃上一顿丰盛的大餐,他那些住在其他城镇的有钱朋友们都会来看他。安东尼奥的爷爷会去伯爵家的厨房帮忙。因为他不光是个好石匠，还是个好厨子。

故事发生在安东尼奥跟着祖父一起到伯爵家的大房子那天，城里来了很多人，要举办一场盛大的宴会，男孩不会做饭，岁数也不够做侍应生。但他能洗盘子和壶，而且他聪明又敏捷，能在其他方面帮忙。

直到要布置餐桌准备开始晚餐，一切都进展得很顺利。突然，餐厅里出现一声巨响，一个男人冲进了厨房，手里拿着几块大理石。他面色苍白，吓得簌簌发抖。

"我该怎么办？我该怎么办？"他大叫。"我把放在桌子中央的雕像打碎了，没有雕像餐桌就没了好看的装饰，伯爵会说什么？"

现在所有的仆人都受到连累了，晚餐最终会搞砸吗？毕竟一切都取决于餐桌精美的布置，伯爵会大发雷霆的。

"啊！我们可怎么办哪？"大家都异口同声地说。

这时小男孩安东尼奥·卡诺瓦放下了手中的锅和壶，走向那个带来麻烦的男人。

"如果再有一个雕像的话，你就能把桌子布置好吗？"他问道。

"当然了。"那个男人答道。"也就是说，只要雕像长度和高度都对的话。"

"你能让我试着再做一个吗？"安东尼奥问道。"也许我能做个替代品。"

那个男人哈哈大笑。"胡说！"他大声说。"你是什么人？你是说你要在一小时之内做好雕像？"

"我叫安东尼奥·卡诺瓦。"小男孩答道。

"让这个孩子试试吧，看他能做什么。"仆人们说道，而且目前也没有其他办法了，那个男人决定让孩子试试。

桌子上有一大块方形黄油，重达两百磅。刚从山里的奶牛厂里送来,又新鲜又干净。安东尼奥手里拿着餐厨刀开始切割雕刻这块黄油。几分钟后,他把黄油塑造成了一个蹲着的狮子的形状,所有的仆人都围拢过来观看。

"太漂亮了!"他们大叫道。"这个比刚才打碎那个好看多了!"

完工后,那个男人把它放到合适的位置上。

他说:"餐桌布置得比我想象的漂亮得多。"

伯爵和朋友们进来用晚餐时,首先他们映入眼帘的就是这头黄色的狮子。

"多么漂亮的艺术品!"他们大声赞叹道。"只有特别伟大的雕塑家才能雕刻出这样的形象,而且用料还是黄油,真是奇思妙想!"然后他们向伯爵询问这是哪位雕塑家的作品。

"说实话,朋友们,"他说,"我跟你们一样吃惊。"然后,他把领班叫来,问他从哪里找来了这么一个漂亮的雕像。

"这是厨房里的一个小男孩一小时前雕刻出来的。"领班回答。

这使伯爵的朋友们更好奇了,伯爵叫仆人把男孩叫进餐厅。

"我的孩子,"他说,"你做出一件连最伟大的艺术家都会为之骄傲的作品。你叫什么名字,谁是你的老师?"

"我叫安东尼奥·卡诺瓦,"男孩说,"我没有老师,不过我的爷爷是个石匠。"

这时,所有的客人都围拢在安东尼奥周围,其中不乏声名显赫的艺术家,他们看出这孩子是个天才,对他的作品赞不绝口。当他们围坐一桌时,让大家最开心的事也就是让安东尼奥与他们坐在一起了。这顿晚餐成了为表示对他的尊敬而举办的盛宴。

就在第二天,伯爵派人请安东尼奥来和他住在一起。雇用当地最好的雕塑家来教他，虽然他的艺术技巧已经相当纯熟。只是现在他不再雕刻黄油了，他雕刻大理石。几年后，安东尼奥·卡诺瓦成了世界上最伟大的雕塑家之一。

Antonio Canova

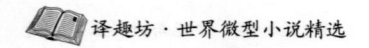

By James Baldwin

A good many years ago there lived in Italy a little boy whose name was Antonio Canova. He lived with his grandfather, for his own father was dead. His grandfather was a stone-cutter, and he was very poor.

Antonio was a puny lad, and not strong enough to work. He did not care to play with the other boys of the town. But he liked to go with his grandfather to the stone-yard. While the old man was busy, cutting and trimming the great blocks of stone, the lad would play among the chips. Sometimes he would make a little statue of soft clay; sometimes he would take hammer and chisel, and try to cut a statue from a piece of rock. He showed so much skill that his grandfather was delighted.

"The boy will be a sculptor someday," he said.

Then when they went home in the evening, the grandmother would say, "What have you been doing today, my little sculptor?"

And she would take him upon her lap and sing to him, or

tell him stories that filled his mind with pictures of wonderful and beautiful things. And the next day, when he went back to the stone-yard, he would try to make some of those pictures in stone or clay.

There lived in the same town a rich man who was called the Count. Sometimes the Count would have a grand dinner, and his rich friends from other towns would come to visit him. Then Antonio's grandfather would go up to the Count's house to help with the work in the kitchen; for he was a fine cook as well as a good stone-cutter.

It happened one day that Antonio went with his grandfather to the Count's great house. Some people from the city were coming, and there was to be a grand feast. The boy could not cook, and he was not old enough to wait on the table; but he could wash the pans and kettles, and as he was smart and quick, he could help in many other ways.

All went well until it was time to spread the table for dinner. Then there was a crash in the dining room, and a man rushed into the kitchen with some pieces of marble in his hands. He was pale, and trembling with fright.

"What shall I do? What shall I do?" he cried. "I have broken the statue that was to stand at the center of the table. I cannot make the table look pretty without the statue. What will the Count say?"

And now all the other servants were in trouble. Was the dinner to be a failure after all? For everything depended on having the table nicely arranged. The Count would be very angry.

"Ah, what shall we do?" they all asked.

Then little Antonio Canova left his pans and kettles, and went up to the man who had caused the trouble.

"If you had another statue, could you arrange the table?" he asked.

"Certainly," said the man, "that is, if the statue were of the right length and height."

"Will you let me try to make one?" asked Antonio. "Perhaps I can make something that will do."

The man laughed. "Nonsense!" he cried. "Who are you, that you talk of making statues on an hour's notice?"

"I am Antonio Canova," said the lad.

"Let the boy try what he can do," said the servants, And so, since nothing else could be done, the man allowed him to try.

On the kitchen table there was a large square lump of yellow butter. Two hundred pounds the lump weighed, and it had just come in, fresh and clean, from the dairy on the mountain. With a kitchen knife in his hand, Antonio began to cut and carve this butter. In a few minutes he had molded it into the shape of a crouching lion; and all the servants crowded around to see it.

"How beautiful!" they cried. "It is a great deal prettier than the statue that was broken."

When it was finished, the man carried it to its place.

"The table will be handsomer by half than I ever hoped to make it," he said.

When the Count and his friends came in to dinner, the first thing they saw was the yellow lion.

"What a beautiful work of art!" they cried. "None but a very great artist could ever carve such a figure; and how odd that he should choose to make it of butter!" And then they asked the Count to tell them the name of the artist.

"Truly, my friends," he said, "this is as much of a surprise to me as to you." And then he called to his head servant, and asked him where he had found so wonderful a statue.

"It was carved only an hour ago by a little boy in the kitchen," said the servant.

This made the Count's friends wonder still more; and the Count bade the servant call the boy into the room.

"My lad," he said, "you have done a piece of work of which the greatest artists would be proud. What is your name, and who is your teacher?"

"My name is Antonio Canova," said the boy, "and I have had no teacher but my grandfather the stone-cutter."

By this time all the guests had crowded around Antonio. There were famous artists among them, and they knew that the lad was a genius. They could not say enough in praise of his work; and when at last they sat down at the table, nothing would please them but that Antonio should have a seat with them; and the dinner was made a feast in his honor.

The very next day the Count sent for Antonio to come and live with him. The best artists in the land were employed to teach him the art in which he had shown so much skill; but now, instead of carving butter, he chiseled marble. In a few years, Antonio Canova became known as one of the greatest sculptors in the world.

小矮马和驴

[英国] 杰克·奥尔索普

罗谢尔和艾玛都狂热地爱马。她俩都住在一个农场附近,所以只要一有机会,就去看农夫的马。她们都没有骑过马,但两人都梦想着有一天能骑上属于自己的小马驰骋。一年一度的儿童诗歌比赛开始了,她们盯着比赛通知,不敢相信自己的眼睛。今年的奖品并不如往常那样无聊——一本书、参观一次博物馆,等等——今年的奖品却是骑小马一日游!

"我们参加吧,好吗,艾玛?"

"你什么意思,罗谢尔?要写一首诗吗?我英语课最差劲了。"

"我也是。不过值得一试,艾玛。想想看,骑马整整一日游啊!"

"可是我们写什么呢?"

"嗯,我要写一首关于小马的诗!"

"我们不能都写关于小马的诗,是吗,罗谢尔?"

"好吧,我告诉你怎么办吧。你写小马,我写……"她怎么也想不出来写什么。艾玛来救援。

"写驴怎么样,罗谢尔?"

"别犯傻了,艾玛。我受不了驴。愚蠢的动物。"

"好吧。罗谢尔,我告诉你:你写小马,我写驴。"

她们要来报名表,开始写诗。几天来,她们努力写诗,找合适的词,试着押韵,绞尽脑汁。最后她俩都有了可以寄的诗。艾玛来到罗谢尔的家。

"快点,罗谢尔,让我听听你写的诗。"

"好吧,不过你也得让我听听你写的才行,艾玛。我想象不出来你能对驴有什么说法!"

"快点。你先来。"

罗谢尔清了清嗓子,开始大声朗读起来。"漂亮的小马:漂亮的小马,套着崭新的马鞍,昂首阔步地一路小跑穿过车水马龙……"

艾玛听到了最后,说这首诗写得真好。接着轮到她了。

"驴:我的脑袋太大,我的耳朵太长,我的腿太短,我的尾巴也长得不像样……"

当罗谢尔听了艾玛整首关于驴的诗后,她说:"你的诗一定会赢。太精彩了!"

"不,"艾玛说。"你的诗比我的诗好多了。我打赌你赢。"两个女孩第一次意识到她俩中只有一个人能赢。这让她们陷入了沉思。她们把诗和报名表都交给了罗谢尔的妈妈,让她把诗装进信封,再放邮筒里,然后就出去玩了。

获胜者收到了一封信:"祝贺你!你的诗在今年的儿童诗歌大赛中获得了一等奖,诗歌将于下周在《汉普郡公报》上发表。请于6月20日周六上午9点到索普里马厩来……"

罗谢尔周六过得很愉快。她只希望艾玛也能和她一起去。事实上,艾玛和她的父母去度假了,她甚至不知道罗谢尔在诗歌比赛中得了奖。罗谢尔还有一件高兴的事:看到她的诗被刊登在当地报纸上。报纸一

与自己和解　才能与世界温柔相处

到，她就迫不及待地翻阅起来。报纸上有一篇关于诗歌比赛和获奖诗歌的报道。开头是：

"我的脑袋太大，我的耳朵太长……"

这不是她写的诗，而是艾玛写的！罗谢尔搞不懂。她妈妈把报名表和诗放进信封里时，一定弄混了。她该怎么面对艾玛呢？她可怎么解释呢？"艾玛，你的诗是最棒的，但骑马一日游的人却是我。"有一阵儿，罗谢尔感到非常难过。于是她对自己说："愚蠢的裁判！真没想到会更喜欢一头蠢驴！"

The Pony and the Donkey

By Jake Allsop

Rochelle and Emma were mad about horses. They both lived near a farm, and visited the farmer's horses whenever they could. Neither of them had ever been on a horse, but each one dreamed of the day when she would have her own pony to ride. When the annual Children's Poetry Competition came round, they stared at the notice in disbelief. Instead of the usual boring prizes—a book, a visit to the museum, etc—the prize this year was a day's pony trekking!

"Let's enter, shall we, Emma?"

"What do you mean, Rochelle? Write a poem? English is my worst subject."

"Same here. But it's worth trying, Em. Just think, a whole day's pony trekking!"

"But what'll we write about?"

"Well, I shall write a poem about a pony!"

"We can't both write about the same thing, can we, Rochelle?"

"Well, I tell you what. You write about a pony, and I'll write about a..." She couldn't think of anything. Emma came to her rescue.

"What about a donkey, Rochelle?"

"Don't be stupid, Emma. I can't stand donkey. Stupid animals."

"All right, Rochelle I tell you what: you write about a pony, and I'll write about a donkey."

They sent for entry forms and set to work. For days, they worked on their poems, seeking the right words, trying to find rhymes, scratching their heads. Finally they both had something to send off. Emma went round to Rochelle's house.

"Come on, Rochelle, let me hear yours."

"All right, but only if you'll let me hear yours, Em. I can't imagine what you found to say about a donkey!"

"Go on. You first."

Rochelle cleared her throat and began to read aloud. "*Pretty little pony: Pretty little pony with a brand new saddle, Trotting through the traffic with its head held high...*"

Emma listened to the end and said how good it was. Then it was her turn.

"*The donkey: My head is too big and my ears are too long, My legs are too short, and my tail is all wrong...*"

When she had heard the whole of Emma's poem about the donkey, Rochelle said: "Yours is bound to win. It's brilliant!"

"No," said Emma. "Yours is much better. I bet you win." For the first time, the two girls realized that only one of them could win. It made them think. They left the poems and entry forms for Rochelle's mother to put into envelopes and post, and went out to play.

The winner got a letter: "Congratulations! Your poem has won first prize in this year's Children's Poetry Competition. It will be published in next week's Hampshire Gazette. Please come to Sopley Stables at 9 am on Saturday 20 June..."

Rochelle had a wonderful day at Saturday. She only wished Emma could have been there, too. In fact, Emma had gone on holiday with her parents, and didn't even know that Rochelle had won the poetry prize. There was still one more treat for Rochelle: seeing her poem printed in the local newspaper. When the paper arrived, she leafed through the pages impatiently. Inside, there was a report of the competition and the winning poem. It began:

"My head is too big and my ears are too long..."

It wasn't her poem, it was Emma's poem! Rochelle couldn't understand it. The entry forms and the poems must have got mixed up when her mother put them in the envelopes. How could she face Emma? What would she say? "Emma, your poem was best, but I was the one who went pony trekking." For a while, Rochelle felt really bad. Then she said to herself: "Stupid judges! Fancy preferring a stupid about donkey!"

幸运的礼服

圣诞节的时候，我戴上了订婚戒指。我和男友交往已快一年，我们都感到是携手步入神圣的婚姻殿堂开始共同生活的时候了。

整个1月我都忙于计划我们将于6月在阿拉巴马州举行的完美婚礼。我和母亲连同两个姐姐前往最近的城市汉斯维尔的一些新娘服装店去选购结婚礼服，这可是我的大日子里至关重要的一个环节。

那段时间，我们母女四人心情愉快地在一起，互相开着傻傻的玩笑。但是等到了下午，气氛就变得严肃起来：还没有我梦想中的结婚礼服的影子。我的两个姐姐都已经准备就此打道回府，改天再到其他城镇去买，但是我迫使她们陪我再多看一家小店。

当我们进入这家满是鲜花香味的精致小店时，我产生了一种很好的预感。

上年纪的店员让我们看了几件美丽的礼服，尺寸适合我穿，价格也都在我的预算之内，但都不是我想要的。

正当我打开店门准备离开之即，孤注一掷的老板娘喊道，在后面库里还有一件礼服，这件礼服很贵，甚至不是我穿的号码，但是也许我还是想看一眼。当她拿出来时，我欣喜地尖叫起来。

就是它啦！

我冲进试衣间，手脚麻利地穿上了礼服。尽管它太大，至少要大上两个尺码,价格也比我预想的要高,我还是说服母亲买下了它。这家店很小,连改衣服的服务都不提供,但是在激动之余,我确信能在家乡把它改好。

然而,只有激动是不够的。星期一早上,当我们那儿的裁缝店告诉我因为礼服上手工缝制的珠子和饰片太多而根本无法改动时,我的天塌下来了。我打电话给卖礼服的那家服装店寻求建议,却只听到了电话的自动应答。

一个朋友给了我镇上一个裁缝的电话,这个裁缝在家里做改衣服的活儿。在绝望之余,我愿意进行任何尝试。于是我决定给她打个电话。

我赶到她位于城镇郊区那幢简朴的小白房子后,她仔细地察看了我的礼服,并让我穿上。她用一把别针将礼服的肩膀处和两侧别上,让我两天后来取衣服。她正是我祈祷的回音。

该去取衣服了,而我却忐忑不安起来。我怎么这么愚蠢,将一件价值1200美元的礼服交到一个一点也不了解的人手里?如果她改坏了怎么办?我甚至不知道她会不会缝扣子。

谢天谢地,我的担心都是多余的。礼服仍跟以前一样美,不过现在我穿上正合适,仿佛它是为我量身定做的一般。我谢过那个令人愉快的女裁缝,并付了她一笔不高的费用。

然而这只是及时解决了一个小问题,更大的问题还在后面。情人节那天,我的未婚夫打来了电话。

"桑迪,我回过味儿来了,我明白自己还没有对婚姻做好准备。"他宣布,那口气一点也不温柔。"在成家之前,我想要出去旅游,体验几年生活。"

他为把取消婚礼的所有麻烦留给我而表示歉意,然后很快离开了这个城镇。

我的世界被颠覆了。我愤怒,心碎,不知道怎么缓过来。然而随着日复一日、月复一月的时光流逝,我熬过去了。

同年的一个秋日,我在超市排队结账的时候,听见有人叫我的名字。我一扭头,看到那个给我改礼服的女裁缝。她很有礼貌地问起我的婚礼,得知被取消后她十分吃惊,但随后表示也许未来会有更好的出现。

我再一次感谢她帮我修改我的结婚礼服,并且向她保证,礼服被我稳妥地收起来了,等待我穿上它挽着我真正的"白马王子"走上红毯的一天。

她眼睛里闪过一道亮光,开始跟我谈起她还是单身的儿子蒂姆。尽管我对再约会没有兴趣,我还是听任她给我安排跟她儿子的约会。

我终于有了自己的夏季婚礼,只不过是在一年以后。我也终于穿上了我梦中的结婚礼服,只不过是站在蒂姆身旁。在随后的18年里,我们携手走过。如果不是因为这件特殊的礼服,我们永远不会相遇。

The Blessed Dress

I got an engagement ring for Christmas. My boyfriend and I had been dating for almost a year and both felt the time was right to join our lives together in holy matrimony.

The month of January was spent planning our perfect Alabama June wedding. My mother, two sisters and I went to Huntsville, the closest town with a selection of bridal shops, to buy the gown that would play the leading role on my special occasion.

We had a wonderful time just being together and sharing silly jokes, but the day soon turned serious by afternoon: still no sign of the dress of my dreams. Both sisters were ready to give up and try another day in another town, but I coerced them into one more boutique.

I had a good feeling as we entered the quaint little shop filled with the scent of fresh flowers.

The elderly clerk showed us several beautiful gowns in my size and price range, but none were right.

As I opened the door to leave, the desperate shop owner announced she had one more dress in the back that was expensive and not even my size, but perhaps I might want to look at it anyway. When she brought it out, I squealed in delight.

This was it!

I rushed to the dressing room and slipped it on. Even though it was at least two sizes too large and more costly than I had anticipated, I talked Mom into buying it. The shop was so small it didn't offer alterations, but my excitement assured me I would be able to get it resized in my hometown.

Excitement wasn't enough. On Monday morning, my world crumbled when the local sewing shop informed me the dress simply could not be altered because of numerous hand-sewn pearls and sequins on the bodice. I called the boutique for suggestions but only got their answering machine.

A friend gave me the number of a lady across town who worked at home doing alterations. I was desperate and willing to try anything, so I decided to give her a call.

When I arrived at her modest white house on the outskirts of town, she carefully inspected my dress and asked me to try it on. She put a handful of pins into the shoulders and sides of my gown and told me to pick it up in two days. She was the answer to my prayers.

When the time came to pick it up, however, I grew skeptical. How could I have been so foolish as to just leave a $1,200 wedding dress in the hands of someone I barely knew? What if she made a mess out of it? I had no idea if she could even sew on a button.

Thank goodness my fears were all for naught. The dress still looked exactly the same, but it now fit as if it had been made especially for me. I thanked the cheerful lady and paid her modest fee.

One small problem solved just in time for a bigger one to emerge. On Valentine's Day, my fiance called.

"Sandy, I've come to the decision that I'm not ready to get married, " he announced, none too gently. "I want to travel and experience life for a few years before settling down."

He apologized for the inconvenience of leaving all the wedding cancellations to me and then quickly left town.

My world turned upside down. I was angry and heartbroken and had no idea how to recover. But days flew into weeks and weeks blended into months. I survived.

One day in the fall of the same year, while standing in line at the supermarket, I heard someone calling my name. I turned around to see the alterations lady. She politely inquired about my wedding, and was shocked to discover it had been called off, but agreed it was probably for the best.

I thanked her again for adjusting my wedding gown, and assured her it was safely bagged and awaiting the day I would wear it down the aisle on the arm of my real "Mister Right".

With a sparkle in her eye, she began telling me about her single son, Tim. Even though I wasn't interested in dating again, I let her talk me into meeting him.

I did have my summer wedding after all, only a year later. And I did get to wear the dress of my dreams—standing beside Tim, the man I have shared the last eighteen years of my life with, whom I would never have met without that special wedding gown.

做风筝的人

[印度] 瑞卡·拉奥

我知道他住在大都市孟买铁道边上的贫民窟一间昏暗、肮脏的小房子里。屋子里没有刷漆，没有电，没有适当的通风设备，甚至没有屋顶。它的存在没有名字，也没有特征。

我第一次见他的时候还不到5岁。那时正值放风筝的季节，我陪着哥哥去买风筝。哥哥去见西塔拉姆，西塔拉姆做的风筝是我们这一片最棒的，不光结实牢固，还很好看。我哥哥想要一只结实的风筝，因为他想参加当地的放风筝大赛。于是西塔拉姆给了他一只非常结实的风筝。但对于我这样天真的孩子来说，给我印象最深的却是那些五彩缤纷的复杂图案，看起来更像是幅拼贴画。虽然哥哥输了那场比赛，但是那只风筝一直在我的记忆当中，还有那个做风筝的人。

于是，在接下来的几年里，我都陪哥哥去做风筝的人那里。我非常乐意看那些风筝，美丽的，艳丽的，它们都是经过精心设计的。风筝都排列在西塔拉姆家的墙上；油灯发出的昏黄的光给风筝原有的颜色镀了一层金色。在我看来，它们都是无价的艺术品，远远超过人们用于修理和购买的价格。在这些风筝中，我找到了一种满足的快乐感觉。

随着年龄的增长，我试着去找更多关于做风筝的人的信息。我发现他有两个儿子和一个女儿,他的妻子死于肺炎,他已经快 50 岁了,他女儿 12 岁的时候就结了婚,他的儿子们也成了家,摆脱了贫民窟的生活,但西塔拉姆孤身一人依旧住在贫民窟里。尽管他做的风筝既有艺术性又有美感,在宫殿和旅馆以及达官贵人的家里,他的风筝随处可见,但他的风筝也能高高地飞翔在天际。他为所有人制作风筝,不论贫富贵贱。

做风筝的人继续他的工作,做更多的风筝,既美丽又绚丽,如昔温暖。他的声誉与日俱隆,远近闻名。他对此置若罔闻,依旧孤身一人住在粗陋的屋子里,做着他的艺术品。

现在,我已经 30 岁了。据我第一次见西塔拉姆已经有 25 年了。他的风筝总是在质问我,让我去更多地探究它们,探究它们的制造者。一直到现在我明白了我想知道什么了。

此时是在 2 月的中旬,正值印度放风筝的季节。大清早 6 点钟,我就在这个时候要去寻找做风筝的人。我明白我一定要去见他。

去找他的路上,我穿过很多肮脏的地方,我的心里百味杂陈,我想转身跑回我那舒适的家,但我知道没有回头路。即使时间还这么早,我看到西塔拉姆已经在忙着做风筝了。我站在窗口,西塔拉姆一如既往地全神贯注于工作,我迷失在他专心致志做风筝的过程中。像是感觉到有人,他抬起头来,我被发现偷窥,很是尴尬,但他一看见是我,便真诚地笑着邀请我进去,虽然他笑的时候,我发现他的牙都掉光了。

"贝塔,我的孩子,你怎么这么早就来啦?"他说着,指了指屋里唯一的椅子示意让我坐下。虽然这把椅子看起来很旧、不太结实的样子。

"老人家,我想知道为什么你做了这么多美丽的风筝,一小部分高价卖给富人,而剩下的大部分低价卖给孩子们。"西塔拉姆似乎被我的问题逗乐了,可能之前从没有人问过他这种问题。

"贝塔,我在风筝中找到了自己的一部分。风筝是我的创造,是我的爱,我用努力和痛苦创造出来的。它们是我爱、痛苦和欢乐的表现。"

"老人家,那你为什么卖给富人的价格那么高?"

听罢,他沉默了一会儿,我看到他沧桑的双眼热泪盈眶。

"因为我需要钱来养活自己,我需要穿衣服。还要买材料做更多的风筝。我的快乐寄托在那些翱翔天际的风筝身上,它们才是真正的我。我在迷失中找到自我。我走不出去,可风筝能代替我走出去。它们代替我挣脱了束缚,自由飞翔。它们带着我的心灵、我的灵魂。要是没有我的风筝,我什么都不是。"

"那美丽又复杂的图案又象征着什么呢?"

"贝塔,那象征着生命的美丽,不论我拥有与否,它们都在我的风筝、我的感觉和我的快乐中。可现在我左眼的白内障正削弱着我的视力,但我很清楚,只要我活着,我就会一直做风筝。因为它们是我唯一的希望,我和我的风筝一起,一起飞翔,一直冲向云霄。也是在欢乐中,在飞翔的欢乐中,我抛弃了自己,我的痛苦,还有我的悲伤。"

我看了看他那湿润的双眼,又看了看他从小因小儿麻痹瘫痪的双腿。我想,我可能明白了。

Kite Maker

By Rekha Rao

I knew that he lived in the slums lining the railway tracks in the metropolis of Mumbai, a small dingy room. It was a room with no paints, no electricity, no proper ventilation or the roof. It was a nameless, faceless existence.

I had met him for the first time when I was barely 5 years old. It had been height of the kite-flying season and I had accompanied my elder brother to buy the kite. He had gone to meet Sitaram who made the best kites in our neighbourhood, the kites that were strong, sturdy and beautiful. My brother had wanted a sturdy kite as he wanted to enter the local kite flying competition. So the kite maker Sitaram had given him a sturdy, strong kite, but what impressed me, an innocent kid, were its intricate, colourful patterns, more like a collage. Although my brother lost the competition, the kite stayed on in my memory, as did the kite maker.

Then for couple of years, I would always accompany my brother to the kite maker. I was always delighted to see those kites, beautiful and rich, that had been so painstakingly done. The kites lined the walls of Sitarams room; the yellow glow of the oil lamp gave a golden shade to the original colors of the kites. They were priceless creations of art for me, so much beyond the values that people fixed and paid for it. I found a feeling of joy, of satisfaction in those kites.

As I grew older I tried to find more about the kite maker. I found that he had 2 sons and a daughter, his wife had died of pneumonia, he was in his late 40s, his daughter had been married when she was 12 years old, also his sons had got married and had moved away from the life in the slums, but Sitaram had stayed on in that slum, in his confinement. Even though his kites, artistic and beautiful, found a place in the interiors of palaces and hotels and bungalows of the rich and famous, his kites also flew high into the sky. The kites of kite maker were for everyone, the rich, and the poor.

And the kite maker went on with his work, the work of making more kites, beautiful, colourful, heart-warming as before, as his fame and his glory went on increasing. Mindless of that, he lived all alone in that clumsy room and went on with his art.

I am 30 years old now. It has been 25 years since I had meet Sitaram for the very first time. His kites had always questioned me, probed me to know more about them, their maker. Now I decided to know exactly what I wanted to know.

It was mid of February, the height of kite flying season in India. It was 6 o'clock in the morning, and that unearthly hour had me going in search of the kite maker. I knew I had to meet him.

The walk to his room had taken me through many filthy places, myriad of emotions filled me, I wanted to turn back and run back to the comforts of my house, but I knew that there was no turning back. Even at such an early hour, I found Sitaram busy with his work of kite making. I stood at the window, lost in the process of kite making as Sitaram went on dedicatedly with his work. Then as if sensing someone, he looked up, I was embarrassed to be caught spying, but on seeing me he invited me in with a toothless, genuine smile.

"Beta, my child, how come you are here at such an early hour?" he said, pointing at the only chair in the room for me to sit. Even that chair appeared fragile and worn-out.

"Baba, I wanted to know why do you make many beautiful kites, yet sell only few for higher prices to the rich people and sell the rest at lower prices to the kids." Sitaram seemed amused at my question; maybe no one ever asked him this kind of questions.

"Beta, I find a part of myself in my kites. My kites are my creations, my love, they are a thing that I have lovingly created with pain and hard work. They are my expressions of love, of pain, of joy."

"Then, Baba, why do you sell some kites for such high price?"

For a moment there was silence, then there were tears in his old eyes.

"Because I do need money to feed myself, cloth myself. And to buy things to create more kites. But my happiness lies in those kites that fly high into the sky and they are the real me. I find myself in my loss. I can't go out, but my kites do that for me. They break free for me; they fly away with freedom, with no restrictions. They take with them my heart and my soul. I would be nothing without them my kites."

"And the beauty, the intricacy, what does it symbolise."

"Beta, it symbolises the beauties of life, those that I can afford and those that I can't have, they are all there in my kites, my feelings, my joys. But now the cataract in my left eye is diminishing my eyesight, but still I know as long as I live my kites will be there, for they are my only hope, my kites and me with them, together we fly, we soar up, up in the sky. And so in its joy, the joy of flying, I lose myself, my pains, my sorrows."

I looked at his misty eyes, then at his legs that had been paralyzed since childhood due to polio. I thought, maybe, I understood.

业余爱好者

[美国] 弗雷德里克·布朗

"我听说一个传闻,"桑斯特罗姆说道,"说你……"他回过头去东张西望地查看在这个小药店里是不是只有他和药店老板两个人。药店老板是一个小个子的男人,年龄从 50 岁到 100 岁都有可能。虽然只有他们两个人,但桑斯特罗姆还是把音量压到了最低:"说你有一种根本查不出来的毒药。"

药店老板点点头。他从柜台里走出来,把店铺的前门锁上,然后走向柜台后面的另一个门口。"我正要休息一下喝杯咖啡。"他说,"跟我一起来喝一杯吧。"

桑斯特罗姆跟着他绕过柜台,然后穿过那个门口来到一间后屋,只见屋里从地板到天花板的架子上摆满了瓶子。药店老板把电咖啡壶插上,找了两只杯子放在桌子上,桌子一边摆着一把椅子。他示意桑斯特罗姆坐在一把椅子上,自己坐在另一把椅子上。"现在,告诉我。你想杀谁?为什么?"他说道。

"这有什么关系吗?"桑斯特罗姆问道,"我付钱不就得了吗?"

药店老板挥挥手打断了他的话。"是的,有关系。你必须有足够理由说服我,让我觉得你配我给你的东西,否则……"他耸耸肩说。

桑斯特罗姆说道:"那好吧。那个人是我的妻子,因为……"他开始讲一个长长的故事。在他快要讲完他的故事之前,电咖啡壶也把咖啡煮开了。药店老板简短地打断了一下,给两人把咖啡倒好。桑斯特罗姆之后讲完了故事。

小个子药店老板点点头说道:"是的,我偶尔也会给出一粒查不出来的毒药。我想给就给,还不收钱,只要那个人该死的话。我已经帮助过许多杀手了。"

"很好,"桑斯特罗姆说,"那么,请你把它给我吧。"

药店老板笑眯眯地对他说:"我已经给你了,在咖啡煮开的时候我就认定你配得到毒药。就像我说的那样,是免费的。但需要付解药的钱。"

桑斯特罗姆脸色霎时变得苍白起来。虽然这完全出乎他的意料,但是他对可能出现的诈骗,或是某种形式的敲诈勒索行为还是有所准备的,于是他当即从口袋里掏出一把手枪。

小个子药店老板咯咯地笑道:"你不敢开枪。开了枪,你还能找到解药吗?"他边说边向那些架子挥了挥手,"在这上千个瓶子里面?或许你会找到一个见效更快、更致命的毒药?如果你认为我是在虚张声势,而你并没有真的中毒的话,那你就动手开枪吧。三个小时之后,毒药一发作你就会知道答案了。"

"解药要多少钱?"桑斯特罗姆低声怒吼道。

"价格相当合理,才1000美元,说到底,人都需要生存,哪怕他的嗜好是阻止谋杀,也没有理由不让他以此赚钱呀,是吧?"

桑斯特罗姆低声咆哮着把手枪放了下来,但放在了触手可及的地方,然后拿出了他的钱包。或许等他拿到解药后,他仍然可以用到那把手枪。他数了10张百元钞票,共1000美元,然后放在桌上。

药店老板没有立即把钱拿起来。他说:"还有一件事情要做,为了我和你太太的安全,你是不是把你之前的意图,也就是谋杀你太太的意图,写一份坦白书?然后你在这里等我出去把这份坦白书寄给我在警局的朋友,他会把它作为证据保存起来,以防你在什么时候真的决定为了那件事要杀害你太太或者我。

"我把坦白书寄出之后,我就安全了,我会回来这里给你解药,我现在给你找纸和笔……

"哦,还有一件事情要做,请帮忙传一下,说我有查不出来的毒药,好吗?当然,我并不坚持要你一定要这样做。谁又能知道呢?桑斯特罗姆先生,如果你有仇人的话,你救的说不定正是你自己的命呢。"

An Amateur

By Fredric Brown

"I heard a rumor," Sangstrom said, "that you—" He turned his head and looked about him to make absolutely sure that he and the druggist were alone in the tiny drugstore. The druggist was a little man who could have been any age from fifty to a hundred. They were alone, but Sangstrom dropped his voice just the same. "that you have a completely undetectable poison."

The druggist nodded. He came around the counter and locked the front door of the shop, then walked toward a doorway behind the counter. "I was about to take a coffee break," he said. "Come with me and have a cup."

Sangstrom followed him around the counter and through the doorway to a back room ringed by shelves of bottles from floor to ceiling. The druggist plugged in an electric coffee pot, found two cups and put them on a table that had a chair on either side of it. He motioned Sangstrom to one of the chairs and took the other himself. "Now," he said, "Tell me. Whom do you want to kill, and why?"

"Does it matter?" Sangstrom asked. "Isn't it enough that I pay for—"

The druggist interrupted him with an upraised hand. "Yes, it matters. I must be convinced that you deserve what I can give you. Otherwise—" he shrugged.

"All right," Sangstrom said. "The whom is my wife. The why—" he started the long story. Before he had quite finished, the coffee pot had finished its task and the druggist briefly interrupted to get the coffee for them. Sangstrom finished his story.

The little druggist nodded. "Yes, I occasionally give out an undetectable poison. I do so freely; I do not charge for it, if I think the case is deserving. I have helped many murderers."

"Fine," Sangstrom said, "Please give it to me, then."

The druggist smiled at him. "I already have. By the time the coffee was ready I had decided that you deserved it. It was, as I said, free. But there is a price for the antidote."

Sangstrom turned pale. But he had expected not this, but the possibility of a double-cross or some form of blackmail. He pulled a pistol from his pocket.

The little druggist chuckled. "You daren't use that. Can you find the antidote?" he waved at the shelves, "among those thousands of bottles? Or would you find a faster, more deadly poison? Or if you think I'm bluffing, that you are not really poisoned, go ahead and shoot. You'll know the answer within three hours when the poison starts to work."

"How much for the antidote?" Sangstrom growled.

"Quite reasonable. A thousand dollars. After all, a man must live. Even if his hobby is preventing murders, there's no reason why he shouldn't make money at it, is there?"

Sangstrom growled and put the pistol down, but within reach, and took out his wallet. Maybe after he had the antidote, he'd still use that pistol. He counted out a thousand dollars in hundred-dollar bills and put them on the table.

The druggist made no immediate move to pick them up. He said: "And one other thing—for your wife's safety and mine. You will write a confession of your intention—your former intention, I hope—to murder your wife. Then you will wait till I go out and mail it to a friend of mine in the police. He'll keep it as evidence in case you ever do decide to kill your wife. Or me, for that matter.

"When that is in the mail it will be safe for me to return here and give you the antidote. I'll get you paper and pen...

"Oh, one other thing—although I do not absolutely insist on it. Please help spread the word about my undetectable poison, will you? One never knows, Mr. Sangstrom. The life you save, if you have any enemies, just might be your own."

一夜惊魂

那是个寒冷的夜晚,莱尼跑夜车时大多都是如此。在利夫·福尔斯干出租车这行已经快 10 年了,公司给他的薪酬不菲,他也认为这份工作相当简单。当然了,莱尼只是个普通人,他喜欢跟人聊天。他是在利弗尔斯长大的,他这辈子阅人无数,确实善于识人。但他不知道今晚要发生的事情远远超出了他的识人本领。

他在路边看到一个人,那人急吼吼地向他招手。他把车停下让那人上来。"谢天谢地,我的车在几个街区外抛锚了,我原本打算走着去上班,没想到这么冷。"他边说边双手搓在一起,哪怕只能搓出一点点的温暖。"你要去哪里?"莱尼看着那人那张通红的脸问道,他突然意识到那人很年轻,也许才二十来岁。

"哦,我在'忙碌的海狸'便利店下车,今晚我要赶去收银。"莱尼注意到那人看起来在为什么事焦虑不安。"你看起来很兴奋。"莱尼说道,但他希望他只是想到了,没有说出来。"嗯,有一个女孩,我那段时间一直想约她,可是她有男朋友,对吧?几天前她和男朋友大吵了一架,我安慰了她,她问我周五有事吗,然后……我就在这里了。"

莱尼偷偷地笑了,他也曾年轻过,也谈过恋爱,看着镜子里自己这张衰老而疲惫的脸,心想岁月可以改变一切。"我爸妈一直催我上大学,你知道的,就像印第安纳大学这样的大学,但这个时候,上大学是我人生中最不想做的事。"男孩说着暖了暖手。"需要暖气开大点吗？"莱尼问道。"不，我不冷了。"男孩没说实话。"忙碌的海狸"便利店就在前面，"嗯，我们到了。"莱尼说着把车停了下来。男孩把车费递过来，再次感谢了莱尼载他。

  莱尼又载了几位乘客，接着在路上看到一个年轻的女孩，年纪和前面第一位乘客差不多。"我借了前男友的车，可你猜怎么着？车没油了。真是跟他一样是个废物。算了，我也不纠结那辆车了，我今晚有约会。请往北派克大道的'忙碌的海狸'便利店开。"说着，女孩补了一下妆。莱尼知道女孩说的是什么人了。"有个可爱的男孩约我到一家豪华餐厅吃饭，即便是本也阻止不了我赴约。"莱尼真想知道这个本会怎么想。他问："要听音乐吗？""哦，可以调到93.3频道吗？"她说着，把粉盒装回小包里。莱尼打开收音机，一首缓慢悲伤的歌传了出来。他把她放在"忙碌的海狸"便利店。"他好像还在工作。"女孩看着收银台前的男孩说道。"哦，好吧，我可以等。谢谢你载我。"说着她把车费递给莱尼，附带相当大的一笔小费。

  他继续往前开，看见一个怒气冲冲的人向他招手。他把车停到那家伙旁边。他上了车。"我猜你今晚过得不太好吧？"莱尼看着那人脸上怒气冲冲的表情问道。"简单扼要地说就是，"男人说，"我给前女友买的生日礼物没有完全合她心意，我睡过头约会迟到了，她就宣布我是个懒鬼，是个废物，这都是不实之词。后来她有了新欢，就甩了我，他俩高中就认识了，她还偷了我的车。"莱尼突然意识到这是谁了。"不管怎样，她的一个朋友告诉我，她今晚要在'忙碌的海狸'便利店和那个家伙见面，我要和她当面对质一下汽车的事。"莱尼微微一笑。"你知道我买车花了多少钱吗？两万美元哪！我从14岁起就开始攒那笔钱啦！"

  他们的车在"忙碌的海狸"便利店停车场停下，那人匆匆下了车，把钱放在了仪表盘上。莱尼开车到乔酒吧附近，遇到一个摇摇晃晃的男人，好像喝醉了。那人确实喝醉了，他慢慢地上了车。"哦，我本来要开车的，但我怕撞到树上。医生常说喝酒会要了我的命。我想这就是我现在一团糟的原因。"经过这个不同寻常一晚的莱尼问道："你这是什么意思？"那人坐立不安地说："我最近经济困难，我要到'忙碌的海狸'那儿去搞些钱来。"莱尼回头看了看那个人，感觉他随时都会吐出来。"你在那儿工作吗？"莱尼问道。"嗯，我想你也可以这么说。"那人咧开嘴笑了，回答道。莱尼不安地坐直了身体。他把那人送到"忙碌的海狸"便利店，当天夜里的工作就结束了。

第二天早上，他正在看报纸，突然看到一篇关于"忙碌的海狸"便利店的报道：**持枪劫匪在本地便利店杀人**——昨天夜里，一名男子和一名女子发生了争执，此前两人已经分手，一名店员介入，这时该便利店的一名旧员工持手枪进店，对该店实施抢劫。警方随后逮捕了这名男子，并证实他在枪击当晚神志不清。负责收银的那位店员心脏中了一枪，差不多可以说当场死亡。劫匪抢劫商品时，那名男子和女子没有受到伤害。这两个人互相安慰，因为死者是他们的朋友。"莱尼放下报纸，心想："真是一夜惊魂啊。"

What a Night

It was a cold night like most of the night's Lenny worked. Lenny had been in the Cab driving business almost 10 years. Leaf Falls Taxi Co. had always paid him a good amount of money for a job he considered pretty simple. Of course Lenny was a common person. He liked to talk. He had grown up in Leaf Falls, in all his life and he had really got to know the people. Little did he know what would happen this night would go beyond just knowing people.

He spotted a man on the side of the street. The man waved eagerly to him. He pulled over and let the man in. "Thank God, my car just broke down a few blocks away and I thought I could walk to work but I didn't realize how cold it was." He said rubbing his hands together to squeeze out even the smallest bit of warmth. "Where you need to go?" Lenny said looking at the man's bright red face. He suddenly realized the man was very young, probably in his twenties.

"Oh, I just need to be dropped off at The Busy Beaver convenience store. I'm running the register tonight." Lenny noticed the man seemed very anxious about something. "You seem excited." Lenny said but wished he had just thought. "Well see there's this girl who I've been trying to date for a while but she had this boyfriend right? So anyway a few nights ago she and her boyfriend got into this huge argument and I comforted her and everything and she asked me if I was doing anything Friday and...well here I am."

Lenny smiled to himself. Lenny had once been young and in love. He looked at his tired old face in the mirror. Time sure had a way of changing things. "My mom and dad keep telling me I gotta go to college you know like I.U., but at this point in my life college is the last thing on my mind." The boy said warming his hands. "Need the heater up some more?" Lenny asked. "Nah, I'm fine." The boy lied. The Busy Beaver was just ahead. "Well here we are." Lenny said stopping the car. The boy handed his fare over and once more thanked Lenny for the ride.

Lenny picked up a few more people before he spotted a young girl in the road looking about the same age as Lenny's first customer. "I borrowed my ex-boyfriend's car and what does it do? Runs out of gas. Just like him a good for nothing. Oh, well I don't care about that car. I've got a date. Busy Beaver convenience store on North Pike Ave, please." The girl said putting on some makeup. Lenny realized who it was. "I got a sweet guy taking me out to a nice restaurant and even Ben can't stop that." Lenny wondered what Ben must be thinking. "So you listen to music?" Lenny asked. "Oh could you turn it on 93.3?" She said putting her makeup back in her purse. Lenny turned on the radio to a slow sad song was playing. He dropped her off at the Busy Beaver. "It looks like he's still working." The girl said looking at the man at the register. "Oh, well I can wait. Thanks for the ride." She said handing him his money and a rather large tip.

He drove down the road and saw an angry man waving for him. He pulled up next to the guy. He got in. "Not a good night I suppose?" Lenny asked looking at the angry expression on the man's face. "That's putting it pretty simple." The man said. "My ex-announces that just because I didn't get her what she exactly wanted for her birthday and that I showed up late for it because I slept in that I'm a lazy good for noting person which I'm not. Afterwards she dumps me for a guy she's known since High School and steals my car." Lenny suddenly realized who this was too. "Anyway one of her friends told me she's meeting the guy at the Busy Beaver tonight I'm gonna confront her about the car." Lenny smiled a small smile. "You know how much that car cost me? 20,000! I've been saving since I was 14!"

They pulled up to the parking lot of the Busy Beaver. The man got out quickly leaving the money on the dashboard. Lenny was driving down near Joe's Bar when he came upon a man staggering as if he were drunk. He was drunk. The man got into the car slowly. "Oh…I would've taken the car but I'm afraid I'd hit a tree. Doctor always said drinking would be the end of me. I guess that's why I'm in this mess." Lenny who had had quite an evening asked, "What you mean?" The man fidgeted, "I've been in financial trouble lately. I'm going on up to the Busy Beaver to get some money." Lenny looked back at the man who looked as if he could vomit any minute. "You work there?" Lenny asked. "Well I guess you could say that." The man replied grinning. Lenny sat up uncomfortably. He dropped off the man at the Busy Beaver and he was done for the night.

The next morning he was reading the paper when he came upon an article about the Busy Beaver. "ARMED ROBBER TAKES LIFE AT LOCAL CONVINENCE STORE. Last night during an argument between a man and a woman who had broken up earlier and a clerk was interrupted when an old employee of the store walked in with a handgun and robbed the place. The police have caught the man and have confirmed that he was not calm on the night of the shooting. The clerk that was working the register took a blow to the heart and died almost instantly. The other two were unharmed as the robber took his goods. The two are comforting each other as the man who was killed had been a friend of theirs." Lenny put down the paper, and thought to himself, "What a night indeed."

命中注定的"爱"

[印度] 皮亚利·迪克西特

里德希玛身穿红色婚纱和阿厘耶门走进新房。这一夜改变了一切，几个小时后她便步入了婚姻阶段，结束了25年的单身生活，从一个女孩变成一个少妇，从一个女儿变成一个儿媳妇。她是童话的虔诚信徒，对婚姻有着无数的梦想和期望。

尽管这是一个包办婚姻，婚礼前她才见到阿厘耶门，但她相信她会拥有自己的爱情故事。身为女孩，她在家一辈子都遭到忽视，她一直执迷地想，自己会得到所爱之人的爱。这世上会有她的专属爱人，一切以她为重。

他俩走进屋里，阿厘耶门锁了门，转身走向她，里德希玛这才有机会欣赏她的丈夫，他的确英俊得像一个王子。阿厘耶门双手合十，对着沉溺在他外貌中的天真的妻子得意扬扬地笑着。

他清了清喉咙，吸引她的注意。"我的妻子啊，你有一整晚的时间来盯着我看，我觉得你该先换衣服，然后我们再继续。"他向她眨了眨眼。里德希玛听了丈夫的话满脸通红，垂下来眼帘，转身从包里拿出东西跑向洗手间换衣服去了。

当她出来的时候，阿厘耶门已经在床上他的那一侧了，他看向她，示意她也到床上来。她绯红了脸,面对着他躺下。他伸出手,她把自己的手放上去,两人迷失在彼此的双眸当中,他缩短了之间的距离,她模仿着也向他移去,他们亲吻,整夜翻云覆雨。

里德希玛在丈夫的臂弯中睁开双眼,想起昨夜的云雨探险,她又激动得满脸通红。她不知道夫妻之间这么早的亲密是不是太快了或者是不是正常,她现在可能还没有爱上她的丈夫,但她确信,她已经在爱他的路上了。想起他是多么温柔地对待自己,她的脸又红了,他眼中或许不是对她的爱,但她在他的眼中看到了对她的关心,对现在而言这就够了,这只是他们的开始,以后的旅程会更加美好。

几天过去了,她此后再也没有见过阿厘耶门的影子。后来她才渐渐了解到他是个酒鬼。他过去常常早上就喝醉了,在家里也常喝多。他是个瘾君子,根本离不开酒,里德希玛让他戒酒的种种努力都是徒劳。

本不应发生的如今都发生了,所有她对爱的梦想都破灭了。那晚过后,他的眼里再也没有爱护和关心了,他惺忪的醉眼中只有一片欲望。那之后,她再没见他清醒过。

可能她没有命中注定的爱情,注定会发生这样的事情。爱情带给她的只是霉运。

几个月过去了,她发现自己怀孕了,这原本应是她人生中最快乐的时段,但9个月过去了,她只是去爱一个从未关心过她的男人,她不确定孩子出生后她要做些什么,她是否能承担起责任来,她是否会爱她的一部分和他的一部分。

不久,她分娩的日子到了,这个丈夫本该陪伴她的日子,可他像往常一样宿醉不醒。她的父母把她送到医院。

等她睁开眼,看到医生对她微笑着,把孩子递到她手里,是个男孩。她泪流满面。他那小手羽毛般的触感,小小的眼睛好奇地看着妈妈,他那小小的、薄薄的嘴唇,在她手里感觉就像是棉球。

　　这一刻她明白了什么是一见钟情,她爱上了自己的小儿子。爱带给她的并不是霉运,这才是它命中注定的方式……

"Love" Meant to Be...

By Pyaali Dixit

Riddhima entered her new house in the red bridal attire with Aryaman. The night has changed it all, in a few hours she entered the marital phase from being single for the 25 years for life, from a girl to a married woman, from a daughter to a daughter-in-law. She had been an ardent believer of fairy tales and had so many dreams, expectations from the marriage.

Although it was an arranged marriage and she met Aryaman just once before marriage but she believed she is going to have her own love story. Being ignored in her family all her life for being a girl, she was just fascinated by the idea that she will be loved back by the person whom she will love. There will be someone just for her and she will be the topmost priority for someone.

They both entered the room, Aryaman locked the door and turned towards her that's when Riddhima got a chance to admire her husband, he was indeed very handsome like a prince. Aryaman folded his hands and smirked on his innocent wife who was lost in him.

He cleared his throat to gain her attention, "You have all the night to stare at me wifey, but I guess you should change first, we will continue after that," and he winked at her. Riddhima flushed at the remark of her husband and lowered her eyes and turned to get her stuff from her bag and ran to washroom to get changed.

When she entered the room Aryaman was already in the bed on his side, he saw her and gestured her to join him on the bed. She blushed and laid down on the bed facing him. He forwarded his hand and she placed her hand on his, both were lost in each other's eyes and he decreased the distance between them, imitating him she also moved forward and they kissed, and the whole night passed in twisting and turning on bed.

Riddhima opened her eyes in the arms of her husband and blushed remembering their night adventures. She didn't knew if it was too fast or normal for couples to be intimate such early, she might not be in love with her husband now but one thing was for sure that she was on the track to love him. She blushed remembering how gently he handled her, it may not be love in his eyes for her but she saw concern in his eyes for her and that was enough for now, it is just the start and their journey will be more beautiful than the start.

Days passed after that and she never saw the glimpse of that Aryaman after that, she came to know after few days that he was an alcoholic. He used to get drunk in the morning itself and used to come drunk in the house. He was an addict and he couldn't leave the alcohol, all attempts of Riddhima were futile in making him leave the alcohol.

It was not supposed to happen like this but happened, all her dreams of love shattered, after that night there was never care or concern in his eyes, it was always a pool of desires in his drooping eyes. She never saw him in his senses after that.

Maybe love was not meant to be for her, it was destined to happen like this. Maybe love was jinxed for her.

Few months passed and she found out she was pregnant, this was supposed to be the happiest phase of her life, but 9 months passed in just trying to love the man who never cared, she was not sure what she was going to do after the child will come in their life, whether she will be able to take the responsibility or whether she will be able to love the part of her, a part of him.

Soon the day also came when she was supposed to give birth to the child, her husband was supposed to be with her at this time but he was not in his senses as usual. She was admitted in hospital by her parents.

When she opened her eyes the doctor smiled at her and gave the child in her hands, it was a boy. She got tears in her eyes. The feathery touch of his hands, his small eyes seeing her mother curiously, his small thin lips, it felt she had cotton ball in her hands.

In that moment she knew what is Love at first sight, she fell in love with her baby boy. Love was not jinxed for her, it was meant to be in this form...

怎样才能活到 200 岁

[加拿大] 斯蒂芬·里柯克

二十年前我认识一个人,名叫吉金斯,这个人有健身的习惯。

他那时每天早上都要洗一个冷水澡,他说这能使毛孔张开;然后他还要再洗一个热水澡,他说这能使毛孔关闭。他这样做为的是能够随心所欲地开合毛孔。

在每天起床穿衣之前,吉金斯总要站在敞开的窗前练习呼吸半个小时。他说这能扩大肺活量。当然他也可以去鞋店用鞋撑子达到这一目的,可说到底,这种窗前练习不用花一分钱,用半个小时又如何?

穿上内衣后,吉金斯接着会把自己像狗一样拴起来做健身运动。他不是前俯,就是后仰,臀部撅得老高老高的,折腾得可来劲儿啦。

无论在哪儿他都能找到些事儿干。他把所有的时间都花在这上面了。在办公室的时候,他一有空就会趴到地板上,看自己能不能用手指把自己撑起来。如果能,他接下来又会试其他方法,一直要到发现某个动作实在做不了才肯罢休。就连午饭后的那点休息时间他都要用来练腹肌,真是快乐极了。

傍晚回到自己房里后,他不是举铁棍、炮弹,就是玩哑铃,还用牙齿咬住天花板上垂下来的什么东西做引体向上。在半英里之外,你都能听到噼里啪啦的声音。他喜欢这样。

整个晚上他有一半时间吊在房上晃来晃去。他说这能使他头脑清醒。在把头脑完全弄清醒后，他就上床睡觉了。第二天一醒来，他又开始再次清醒头脑。

吉金斯如今死了。他当然是一个先驱者，不过他因哑铃而英年早逝的事，并没有阻止一整代年轻人踏着他的足迹继续前进。

他们都成了健身癖的奴隶。

他们都使自己成了讨厌鬼。

他们在常人难以忍受的时间起床。他们穿着傻傻的套装在早饭前跑马拉松。他们光着脚丫互相追逐，双脚沾满露水。他们猎取新鲜空气。他们为胃蛋白酶伤透脑筋。他们不愿吃肉，因为肉里含氮太多。他们不愿吃水果，因为水果里根本不含氮。他们更喜欢蛋白质、淀粉和氮，却不愿吃馅饼和面包。他们不愿从水龙头直接喝水。他们不愿吃罐装沙丁鱼。他们不愿吃装在桶里的牡蛎。他们不愿喝装在玻璃杯里的牛奶。他们害怕各种各样的酒精。是的，先生，就是怕。真是些"怕死鬼"！

尽管他们对这些细枝末节这么在意，可还是患上了某种简单的老式病，跟别人死得也没有什么两样。

如今这一类人怎么着都与长寿无缘。他们是南辕北辙了。

听我说，你是不是真的想特别长寿，真的想享受美妙、绿色环保、精力充沛、值得夸耀的晚年，同时不用回忆从前招邻居厌烦呢？

那就停止这种愚蠢的行为。就此打住。早上最好在合适的时间起床。没到非起床不可不要起来，犯不着提前。如果你是11点上班，那就10点半起床。有新鲜空气就尽情呼吸吧。不过这东西现在早已绝迹。如果真还有的话，那就花五分钱买上满满一热水瓶，把它放在食橱架上。如果你是早上7点上班，提前10分钟起床就可以，但不要自欺欺人地说你喜欢这样。这不是一件让人高兴的事，你也心知肚明。

另外，放弃洗冷水澡什么的，你小时候都不这样做，现在也犯不着当这种傻瓜。假如你必须洗澡（你其实真不需要），那就用温水吧。从冷飕飕的床上爬起来，跑去洗个热水澡完胜洗冷水澡。不管怎样，不要为你泡过的澡或洗过的"淋浴"吹牛，好像世界上只有你洗过澡似的。

关于这一点就说这么多。

接下来我们谈谈细菌和杆菌的问题。不要害怕它们。有这点就够了。仅此而已，一旦你做到了这一点，那你就再也无须忧心忡忡了。

如果你遇到一个杆菌，径直走上去，直视它的眼睛。如果有一个杆菌飞进了你的房间，用帽子或毛巾抽打它。抽打它的脖子和胸部之间的位置，能多狠就多狠。过不了多久它就会厌倦的。

不过，说老实话，要是你不害怕它的话，杆菌其实是完全安静而且无害的。跟它聊聊天吧。对它说："躺下。"它会懂。我曾经养过一个杆菌，名叫"费多"，我干活的时候，它会走过来躺在我的脚边。我还从没结识过比它更重情义的伴侣。在它被一辆汽车轧死之后，我把它埋在了花园里，悲痛万分。

（我承认这么说有点夸张。我真的不记得它的名字，它说不定叫"罗伯特"。）

要明白，所谓霍乱、伤寒和白喉是由细菌和杆菌引起的，这不过是现代医学流行一时的说法而已，完全是胡说八道。霍乱是由腹部剧疼引起的，白喉则是试图治疗喉痛的结果。

现在我们来谈谈食物的问题。

想吃什么就吃什么好啦。敞开肚子吃吧。对，大吃特吃。一直吃到你要摇摇晃晃才能走到房子的那一头，一直吃到要用沙发靠垫撑住身子才行。爱吃什么就吃什么好啦，直吃到再也吃不动了为止。唯一要考虑的是，你能不能买得起。你买不起，就别吃。还有，听着——别担心你的食物里是否含有淀粉、蛋白质、麸质或氮元素。假如你实在蠢笨至极，非要吃这些东西，那就去买吧，想吃多少就吃多少。可以去洗衣店买一大袋（浆洗衣服的）淀粉来，一次吃个够。吃完之后再大喝一顿胶水，外加一小勺波特兰水泥。这能把你黏得牢牢的，非常瓷实。

如果你喜欢氮，可以到药店的苏打柜台买一大听来，用吸管好好享受一番。只是不要以为这些东西可以和你别的食物混在一起吃。通常的食品中可没有氮、磷或蛋白。在任何一个体面的家庭里，所有这些东西在摆上餐桌之前早就被冲洗在厨房的洗碗槽里了。

最后再就新鲜空气和锻炼的事说一句。不要为它们任何一样烦恼。把你的房间装满新鲜空气，然后关起窗户把它贮藏好，能保存好多年呢。不管怎样，不要每时每刻都用你的肺。让它休息休息吧。至于说锻炼，如果你非锻炼不可的话，那就去锻炼并且忍受它吧。不过要是你有钱雇得起别人为你打棒球、跑步或进行其他锻炼，而你坐在阴凉处吞云吐雾坐享其成——天哪，夫复何求？

How to Live to Be 200

By Stephen Leacock

Twenty years ago I knew a man called Jiggins, who had the Health Habit.

He used to take a cold plunge every morning. He said it opened his pores. After it he took a hot sponge. He said it closed the pores. He got so that he could open and shut his pores at will.

Jiggins used to stand and breathe at an open window for half an hour before dressing. He said it expanded his lungs. He might, of course, have had it done in a shoe-store with a boot stretcher, but after all it cost him nothing this way, and what is half an hour?

After he had got his undershirt on, Jiggins used to hitch himself up like a dog in harness and do Sandow exercises. He did them forwards, backwards, and hind-side up.

He could have got a job as a dog anywhere. He spent all his time at this kind of thing. In his spare time at the office, he used to lie on his stomach on the floor and see if he could lift himself up with his knuckles. If he could, then he tried some other way until he found one that he couldn't do. Then he would spend the rest of his lunch hour on his stomach, perfectly happy.

In the evenings in his room he used to lift iron bars, cannon-balls, heave dumb-bells, and haul himself up to the ceiling with his teeth. You could hear the thumps half a mile. He liked it.

He spent half the night slinging himself around his room. He said it made his brain clear. When he got his brain perfectly clear, he went to bed and slept. As soon as he woke, he began clearing it again.

Jiggins is dead. He was, of course, a pioneer, but the fact that he dumb-belled himself to death at an early age does not prevent a whole generation of young men from following in his path.

They are ridden by the Health Mania.

They make themselves a nuisance.

They get up at impossible hours. They go out in silly little suits and run Marathon heats before breakfast. They chase around barefoot to get the dew on their feet. They hunt for ozone. They bother about pepsin. They won't eat meat because it has too much nitrogen. They won't eat fruit because it hasn't any. They prefer albumen and starch and nitrogen to huckleberry pie and doughnuts. They won't drink water out of a tap. They won't eat sardines out of a can. They won't use oysters out of a pail. They won't drink milk out of a glass. They are afraid of alcohol in any shape. Yes, sir, afraid. "Cowards."

And after all their fuss they presently incur some simple old-fashioned illness and die like anybody else.

Now people of this sort have no chance to attain any great age. They are on the wrong track.

Listen. Do you want to live to be really old, to enjoy a grand, green, exuberant, boastful old age and to make yourself a nuisance to your whole neighbourhood with your reminiscences?

Then cut out all this nonsense. Cut it out. Get up in the morning at a sensible hour. The time to get up is when you have to, not before. If your office opens at eleven, get up at ten-thirty. Take your chance on ozone. There isn't any such thing anyway. Or, if there is, you can buy a thermos bottle full for five cents, and put it on a shelf in your cupboard. If your work begins at seven in the morning, get up at ten minutes to, but don't be liar enough to say that you like it. It isn't exhilarating, and you know it.

Also, drop all that cold-bath business. You never did it when you were a boy. Don't be a fool now. If you must take a bath (you don't really need to), take it warm. The pleasure of getting out of a cold bed and creeping into a hot bath beats a cold plunge to death. In any case, stop gassing about your tub and your "shower", as if you were the only man who ever washed.

So much for that point.

Next, take the question of germs and bacilli. Don't be scared of them. That's all. That's the whole thing, and if you once get on to that you never need to worry again.

If you see a bacilli, walk right up to it, and look it in the eye. If one flies into your room, strike at it with your hat or with a towel. Hit it as hard as you can between the neck and the thorax. It will soon get sick of that.

But as a matter of fact, a bacilli is perfectly quiet and harmless if you are not afraid of it. Speak to it. Call out to it to "lie down". It will understand. I had a bacilli once, called Fido, that would come and lie at my feet while I was working. I never knew a more affectionate companion, and when it was run over by an automobile, I buried it in the garden with genuine sorrow.

(I admit this is an exaggeration. I don't really remember its name; it may have been Robert.)

Understand that it is only a fad of modern medicine to say that cholera and typhoid and diphtheria are caused by bacilli and germs; nonsense. Cholera is caused by a frightful pain in the stomach, and diphtheria is caused by trying to cure a sore throat.

Now take the question of food.

Eat what you want. Eat lots of it. Yes, eat too much of it. Eat till you can just stagger across the room with it and prop it up against a sofa cushion. Eat everything that you like until you can't eat any more. The only test is, can you pay for it? If you can't pay for it, don't eat it. And listen—don't worry as to whether your food contains starch, or albumen, or gluten, or nitrogen. If you are a damn fool enough to want these things, go and buy them and eat all you want of them. Go to a laundry and get a bag of starch, and eat your fill of it. Eat it, and take a good long drink of glue after it, and a spoonful of Portland cement. That will gluten you, good and solid.

If you like nitrogen, go and get a druggist to give you a canful of it at the soda counter, and let you sip it with a straw. Only don't think that you can mix all these things up with your food. There isn't any nitrogen or phosphorus or albumen in ordinary things to eat. In any decent household all that sort of stuff is washed out in the kitchen sink before the food is put on the table.

And just one word about fresh air and exercise. Don't bother with either of them. Get your room full of good air, then shut up the windows and keep it. It will keep for years. Anyway, don't keep using your lungs all the time. Let them rest. As for exercise, if you have to take it, take it and put up with it. But as long as you have the price of a hack and can hire other people to play baseball for you and run races and do gymnastics when you sit in the shade and smoke and watch them—great heavens, what more do you want?

田 岛

从前，有一个博学多闻的浪人，名叫田岛修。他正取道东海道去往京都。（东海道即东海之路，从京都到江户的一条著名的高速公路，也指它穿过的一个县城。）一天，在尾张国的名古屋市，他遇见了一位同样云游的和尚，于是同他攀谈了起来。两人目的地一致，于是决定结伴而行。舟车劳顿，他们用各式各样的话题驱赶着旅途的疲劳。渐渐地，两人变得亲密无间，谈话间也不再避讳隐私话题。和尚十分信任他的伙伴，便把他此行的目的告诉了田岛。

"在过去的一段时间，"他说，"我怀揣一个心愿，这个心愿占据了我的全部思想；因为我一心想建造一座神圣的佛像，以纪念佛陀。我带着这个心愿走遍了各个县城，收集捐赠，而且（谁知道是多么劳累呢？）我相信，我们已经成功地募集到了两百盎司的银子，足以建造一座漂亮的青铜雕像。"

有句谚语是怎么说的？"怀揣宝石的，必带毒药。"浪人一听见和尚的话，心中的邪念就陡然而起，他心想："人的生命，从母腹到坟墓，都是由好运气和坏运气组成的。这是我，将近40岁，一个云游者，没有一个人需要我，甚至没有在世界上继续生活的希望。可以肯定的是，这似乎是一种耻辱；然而，如果我能偷到这个和尚所吹嘘的钱，我就可以安逸地度过余生了。"于是他开始琢磨，他如何才能达到目的。但和尚并没有猜到他的伙伴思想上的变化，而是兴高采烈地继续前行，直到他们到达了宽纳镇。这里有一个海湾，在渡船上横渡，凑够20到30名乘客就一起启程；这两个旅行者上了其中的一条船。船行程大约过了一半，发生了一件事，事发突然，和尚不得不到船的另一边，浪人跟在他后面，趁没人注意的时候绊倒了他，把他猛推到海里。船夫和乘客听见了水声，看见和尚在水中挣扎，他们很害怕并且尽力救他。但是顺风顺水，船上的帆鼓鼓的，船急速地行驶，所以他们很快就离溺水的人几百码远了，和尚在船还没转过来救他之前就沉了下去。

看到这一幕，浪人装出悲痛欲绝又无比沮丧的样子，对同行的乘客们说："我们刚刚失去的那位和尚，他是我的表哥，他要去京都，去拜访他赞助人的神龛；我正好在那里有业务，所以我们决定一起旅行。现在，唉！不幸的是，我表哥死了，就剩下我一个人了。"

他说得那么动情，哭声那么夸张，所以乘客们相信了他的话，他们同情并试图安慰他。浪人对船夫说："我们理应向当局报告这件事，但由于我时间紧迫，这件事也可能给你们带来麻烦，也许我们现在最好不要声张。我马上去京都，告诉我表哥的赞助人，并把这件事的原委写信告知家里。"接着，他转向其他乘客，补充道："先生们，你们觉得怎么样？"

乘客们自然很愿意不让这件事妨碍他们继续旅行。大家异口同声地同意了浪人的建议，于是事情就这样解决了。当他们终于到了岸边，所有人下了船都各走各的路了。只有浪人心里大喜过望，他拿着云游和尚的行李，与自己的行李放在一起，继续前往京都的旅程。

到达首都京都后，浪人将自己的名字从修改为黑田，放弃了武士的身份，改为经商，用死去的和尚的钱做生意。他靠着投机发财，开始积攒大量的财富，安逸地生活着，斩断与过去的联系；随着时间的推移,他娶了一个妻子,妻子给他生了一个孩子。

日子一天天、一月月地就这样过去了,直到一个晴朗的夏夜,也就是和尚死后的三年左右,黑田走出自家的阳台,享受着凉爽的空气和美丽的月光。他感到无聊和孤独,开始思考各种各样的事情,突然间,很久以前做过的谋杀和盗窃的事,生动地浮现在他的记忆中。他心中暗想:"这就是我,我靠着偷来的钱变得越来越富有,身体也发福了。从那以后,我一切都好了;然而,如果我不是穷人,我就不会变成谋杀者和小偷。悲哀降临到我身上!真可惜!"当他在脑子里思考这件事的时候,一种自责的感觉涌上了他的心头,尽管他已经功成名就。当他的良心受到这样的谴责时,他突然惊奇地发现花园里一棵杉树旁有一个站着的人的模糊轮廓;他更加仔细地看了看,发现这个人形销骨立,眼圈深陷,双目无神,他认出了在他面前的这个可怜的鬼就是他所认识的那个和尚,那个被他扔进海里的和尚。他吓得直打寒战,又看了一眼,看见和尚一脸讥笑地望着他。他本可以逃到房子里,但鬼魂伸出它枯萎的胳膊,紧紧抓住他的后颈,对他怒目而视,有复仇的眼神、可怕的神态,这是无法形容的恐怖,任何普通人都会吓得晕倒。尽管黑田现在是一个商人,但他曾经当过兵,不那么容易被吓倒,所以他摆脱了鬼魂,跳到房间里去寻找他的匕首,勇敢地对着周围乱打一气;尽管他打了一阵,那鬼魂还是消失在空气中,躲过了他的打击,突然又出现了,最后又消失了。从那时起,黑田便寝食难安,日夜被鬼魂缠扰。

最后,由于这一让人心烦的事没完没了,黑田终于病倒了,嘴里不停地咕哝着:"哦,不幸!痛苦!云游和尚来折磨我了!"家里的人听见他的哀号和胡闹,都以为他疯了,就叫了一个医生来,医生给他开了处方。但是药丸和药水都不能治愈黑田,他的奇怪病症很快成了邻里街坊茶余饭后的谈资。

现在，这个故事碰巧传到了一个住在另一条街上的云游和尚的耳中。当和尚听到这些细节的时候，他严肃地摇了摇头，仿佛他了解这件事的来龙去脉似的，然后派一个朋友到黑田家里去，说一个住在附近的云游和尚听到了他的病情，如果没有那么严重的话，他可以通过祈祷来治病。黑田的妻子被她丈夫的病折磨得半死，一刻也没耽误，立刻派人去请和尚，把他带进了病人的房间。

但黑田一见到和尚就大声喊："救命！救命！那个云游和尚又来折磨我了。饶命！饶命！"他把头藏在被单下面，惊恐万状，浑身发抖。和尚就把所有礼物都从房里拿出来，把嘴贴近黑田的耳朵，低声说："三年前，在宽纳渡口，你把我扔到水里，你肯定还记得吧？"

黑田说不出话来，只是恐惧得瑟瑟发抖。

"幸运的是，"和尚继续说道，"我小时候就学会了游泳和潜水，于是我游上了岸，在云游四方以后，成功地为佛陀立了一座铜像，从而实现了我内心的愿望。在我回家的路上，我恰好住在另一条街上，在那里听到了你不可思议的病痛。我以为我能猜出它的原因，就来看你，我很高兴我没有弄错。你行了可憎的事，可是，我不是和尚吗？我不就是要原谅这世上的恶事吗？我忍受恶毒不就是善吗？因此，你要悔改，摒弃你的恶行。看到你这样做，我应该尊重幸福的高度。现在，好好高兴起来，看着我的脸，你会发现我真的是个活人，没有变成复仇的妖怪来折磨你。"

黑田明白不用对付鬼魂了，和尚的善良感化了他，他痛哭失声，回答说："真的，我不知道该说什么。我在疯狂中，试图杀了你，抢劫你。从那以后，命运就对我友好了，但是我越富有，我就越强烈地感觉到自己是多么邪恶，就越预见到我的受害者有朝一日会报复我。我被这个想法所困扰，我害怕了，直到有一天晚上，我看见了你的鬼魂，便病倒了。但是你是怎么设法逃脱,还活到现在,这真令我难以置信。"

"一个有罪的人,"和尚笑着说,"听到风的沙沙声或是鹳喙的咕噜声,他都会瑟瑟发抖;谋杀者的良心一直在折磨着他,直到他看到了子虚乌有的东西。贫穷驱使一个人犯罪,犯罪的人在财富中忏悔。孟子说,人之初,性本善,后来被环境腐蚀,这是多么真实啊!"

他就这样侃侃而谈,而黑田早就为自己的罪行忏悔了,他请求宽恕,给了和尚一大笔钱,说:"这其中的一半是我三年前从你那里偷来的,另一半是我恳求你接受作为利息或礼物。"

起初,和尚拒绝了这笔钱,但黑田坚持要他接受,还竭尽所能挽留他,不过没有成功,因为和尚要继续云游,于是他就把这笔钱给了贫穷和衣食无着的人。至于黑田本人,他很快就摆脱了疾病,从此与所有人和平相处,在国内外受到尊敬,并一直致力于善行和慈善事业。

TAJIMA

Once upon a time, a certain ronin, Tajima Shume by name, an able and well-read man, being on his travels to see the world, went up to Kyoto by the Tokaido. (The road of the Eastern Sea, the famous highroad leading from Kyoto to Yedo. The name is also used to indicate the provinces through which it runs.) One day, in the neighbourhood of Nagoya, in the province of Owari, he fell in with a wandering priest, with whom he entered into conversation. Finding that they were bound for the same place, they agreed to travel together, beguiling their weary way by pleasant talk on diverse matters; and so by degrees, as they became more intimate, they began to speak without restraint about their private affairs; and the priest, trusting thoroughly in the honour of his companion, told him the object of his journey.

"For some time past," said he, "I have nourished a wish that has engrossed all my thoughts; for I am bent on setting up a molten image in honour of Buddha; with this object I have wandered through various provinces collecting alms, and (who knows by what weary toil?) we have succeeded in amassing two hundred ounces of silver—enough, I trust, to erect a handsome bronze figure."

What says the proverb? "He who bears a jewel in his bosom bears poison." Hardly had the ronin heard these words of the priest than an evil heart arose within him, and he thought to himself, "Man's life, from the womb to the grave, is made up of good and of ill luck. Here am I, nearly forty years old, a wanderer, without a calling, or even a hope of advancement in the world. To be sure, it seems a shame; yet if I could steal the money this priest is boasting about, I could live at ease for the rest of my days." And so he began casting about how best he might compass his purpose. But the priest, far from guessing the drift of his comrade's thoughts, journeyed cheerfully on till they reached the town of Kuana. Here there is an arm of the sea, which is crossed in ferry-boats, that start as soon as some twenty or thirty passengers are gathered together; and in one of these boats the two travellers embarked. About half-way across, the priest was taken with a sudden necessity to go to the side of the boat; and the ronin, following him, tripped him up while no one was looking, and flung him into the sea. When the boatmen and passengers heard the splash, and saw the priest struggling in the water, they were afraid, and made every effort to save him; but the wind was fair, and the boat running swiftly under the bellying sails; so they were soon a few hundred yards off from the drowning man, who sank before the boat could be turned to rescue him.

When he saw this, the ronin feigned the utmost grief and dismay, and said to his fellow-passengers, "This priest, whom we have just lost, was my cousin; he was going to Kyoto, to visit the shrine of his patron; and as I happened to have business there as well, we settled to travel together. Now, alas! by this misfortune, my cousin is dead, and I am left alone."

He spoke so feelingly, and wept so freely, that the passengers believed his story, and pitied and tried to comfort him. Then the ronin said to the boatmen: "We ought, by rights, to report this matter to the authorities; but as I am pressed for time, and the business might bring trouble on yourselves as well, perhaps we had better hush it up for the present; I will at once go on to Kyoto and tell my cousin's patron, besides writing home about it. What think you, gentlemen?" added he, turning to the other travellers.

They, of course, were only too glad to avoid any hindrance to their onward journey, and all with one voice agreed to what the ronin had proposed; and so the matter was settled. When, at length, they reached the shore, they left the boat, and every man went his way; but the ronin, overjoyed in his heart, took the wandering priest's luggage, and putting it with his own, pursued his journey to Kyoto.

On reaching the capital, the ronin changed his name from Shume to Tokubei, and giving up his position as a samurai, turned merchant, and traded with the dead man's money. Fortune favouring his speculations, he began to amass great wealth, and lived at his ease, denying himself nothing; and in course of time he married a wife, who bore him a child.

Thus the days and months wore on, till one fine summer's night, some three years after the priest's death, Tokubei stepped out on the veranda of his house to enjoy the cool air and the beauty of the moonlight. Feeling dull and lonely, he began musing over all kinds of things, when on a sudden the deed of murder and theft, done so long ago, vividly recurred to his memory, and he thought to himself, "Here am I, grown rich and fat on the money I wantonly stole. Since then, all has gone well with me; yet, had I not been poor, I had never turned assassin nor thief. Woe betide me! What a pity it was!" And as he was revolving the matter in his mind, a feeling of remorse came over him, in spite of all he could do. While his conscience thus smote him, he suddenly, to his utter amazement, beheld the faint outline of a man standing near a fir-tree in the garden; on looking more attentively, he perceived that the man's whole body was thin and worn, and the eyes sunken and dim; and in that poor ghost that was before him he recognised the very priest whom he had thrown into the sea at Kuana. Chilled with horror, he looked again, and saw that the priest was smiling in scorn. He would have fled into the house, but the ghost stretched forth its withered arm, and clutching the back of his neck, scowled at him with a vindictive glare and a hideous ghastliness of mien so unspeakably awful that any ordinary man would have swooned with fear. But Tokubei, tradesman though he was, had once been a soldier, and was not easily matched for daring; so he shook off the ghost, and leaping into the room for his dirk, laid about him boldly enough; but strike as he would, the spirit, fading into the air, eluded his blows, and suddenly reappeared only to vanish again; and from that time forth Tokubei knew no rest, and was haunted night and day.

At length, undone by such ceaseless vexation, Tokubei fell ill, and kept muttering, "Oh, misery! misery! the wandering priest is coming to torture me!" Hearing his moans and the disturbance he made, the people in the house fancied he was mad, and called in a physician, who prescribed for him. But neither pill nor potion could cure Tokubei, whose strange frenzy soon became the talk of the whole neighbourhood.

Now it chanced that the story reached the ears of a certain wandering priest who lodged in the next street. When he heard the particulars, this priest gravely shook his head as though he knew all about it, and sent a friend to Tokubei's house to say that a wandering priest, dwelling hard by, had heard of his illness, and were it never so grievous, would undertake to heal it by means of his prayers; and Tokubei's wife, driven half wild by her husband's sickness, lost not a moment in sending for the priest and taking him into the sick man's room.

But no sooner did Tokubei see the priest than he yelled out, "Help! help! Here is the wandering priest come to torment me again. Forgive! forgive!" And hiding his head under the coverlet, he lay quivering all over. Then the priest turned all present out of the room, put his mouth to the affrighted man's ear, and whispered: "Three years ago, at the Kuana ferry, you flung me into the water; and well you remember it."

But Tokubei was speechless, and could only quake with fear.

"Happily," continued the priest, "I had learned to swim and to dive as a boy; so I reached the shore, and after wandering through many provinces, succeeded in setting up a bronze figure to Buddha, thus fulfilling the wish of my heart. On my journey homeward, I took a lodging in the next street, and there heard of your marvellous ailment. Thinking I could divine its cause, I came to see you, and am glad to find I was not mistaken. You have done a hateful deed; but am I not a priest, and have I not forsaken the things of this world, and would it not ill become me to bear malice? Repent, therefore, and abandon your evil ways. To see you do so I should esteem the height of happiness. Be of good cheer, now, and look me in the face, and you will see that I am really a living man, and no vengeful goblin come to torment you."

Seeing he had no ghost to deal with, and overwhelmed by the priest's kindness, Tokubei burst into tears, and answered, "Indeed,

indeed, I don't know what to say. In a fit of madness I was tempted to kill and rob you. Fortune befriended me ever after; but the richer I grew, the more keenly I felt how wicked I had been, and the more I foresaw that my victim's vengeance would some day overtake me. Haunted by this thought, I lost my nerve, till one night I beheld your spirit, and from that time fell ill. But how you managed to escape, and are still alive, is more than I can understand."

"A guilty man," said the priest, with a smile, "shudders at the rustling of the wind or the chattering of a stork's beak; a murderer's conscience preys upon his mind till he sees what is not. Poverty drives a man to crimes which he repents of in his wealth. How true is the doctrine of Mencius, that the heart of man, pure by nature, is corrupted by circumstances!"

Thus he held forth; and Tokubei, who had long since repented of his crime, implored forgiveness, and gave him a large sum of money, saying, "Half of this is the amount I stole from you three years since; the other half I entreat you to accept as interest, or as a gift."

The priest at first refused the money; but Tokubei insisted on his accepting it, and did all he could to detain him, but in vain; for the priest went on his way, and bestowed the money on the poor and needy. As for Tokubei himself, he soon shook off his disorder, and thenceforward lived at peace with all men, revered both at home and abroad, and ever intent on good and charitable deeds.

最后一次送货

有一对富有的夫妇要在家里举办一场盛大的新年派对。于是，他们来到一家价格昂贵且不打折的市场，采购派对所需的物品。他们希望保持较高的生活水平，所以并不介意为自己需要的东西多花些钱。

要买的东西都买了，于是，他们叫来一名搬运工帮他们把买到的所有东西送回家。这名搬运工年龄很大，看起来病歪歪的，衣衫褴褛，似乎生活不能自理。

他们向这名搬运工询问了送货到家的费用。这位老搬运工仅给出了20美元的报价，这个价格远远低于将这一车货物送至这对夫妇家中的市场价格。

然而，这对夫妇还是与这名搬运工讨价还价起来，并最终将价格确定为15美元。这名搬运工为了一顿饭要拼命赚钱，所以不会拒绝任何一次能够赚到钱的机会。

这对夫妇非常开心地回味着刚刚他们在与这名可怜的搬运工讨价还价时的精彩表现，他们预付了搬运工15美元，提供了送货地址，然后离开了。他们回到家后，一小时过去了，两个小时过去了，但还是不见搬运工送货上门。

妻子开始对丈夫发起火来："我告诉过你多少遍了，不要相信这种人，你就是把我的话当成耳旁风。这种人每天赚到的钱都不够吃饱饭，你竟然把我们为盛大派对买的东西全部交给了他。我确信，他肯定是带着咱们的东西跑路了，不可能送货上门了。我们得马上回市场弄清楚那名搬运工的底细，然后去警察局报警，准备投诉他。"

　　夫妇二人离开家前往市场。在途中，就在距离市场不远的地方，他们看到另一名搬运工。他们拦住他询问那名老搬运工的情况，但很快他们就注意到这名搬运工的手推车里放的正是他们买的东西！妻子愤怒地问他："那个老贼在哪里？这是我们的东西，他本应该把这些东西送到我家的。看来你们这些贼想要偷走我们的东西，然后转手卖掉。"

　　这个搬运工回答说："夫人，请冷静。那个可怜的老人上个月就生病了。他每天赚的钱都不够吃一顿饭。他在为你们送货的途中因为饿着肚子又体弱多病，在这个炎热的中午，实在没有力气继续送货了。他倒下了，递给我15美元。他对我说的最后一句话是：'我已经收了人家的送货预付款，请拿着这些钱，帮我把货送到这个地址吧。'"

　　"夫人，他又饿又穷，但他是一个诚实的人。我正在帮老人把最后一次货送出去，正往您家送货呢。"搬运工说。听到这些话，丈夫眼睛里涌出了泪花，而他的妻子感到非常羞愧，甚至没有勇气去看她的丈夫一眼。

　　寓意：诚信与阶层无关。我们要尊重每一个人，不管他是不是有钱有势。让每个人都能得到他应得的，这是一件永远值得称道的事情。

The Last Delivery

There was a rich couple who was throwing a big new year party at their house. So they went shopping at a market where everything was of high cost and had a fixed price. They wanted to maintain their high living standards so didn't mind paying a lot for the things they needed.

After purchasing everything they wanted, they called a porter to carry everything and drop it off at their home. The porter who came was of an old age, not very healthy looking. His clothes were torn, and he looked as if he wasn't even able to meet his daily needs.

They asked the porter about the charge for delivering the goods at their home. The old porter quoted a mere $20, a price well below the market rate for delivering goods with his cart at the couple's home.

Yet, the couple argued and bargained with the porter, and finally, he settled for $15. The porter was struggling to make money for every single meal, so he needed anything he could earn.

The couple was very happy thinking about how well they had

bargained with the poor porter, paid him $15 in advance and left after giving the porter their address for delivery. They reached their home and an hour passed, two hours passed, but the porter still hadn't delivered their stuff.

  The wife started to get angry at her husband, "I always tell you to not to trust such a person but still, you never listen to me. Such a person is not even able to earn enough money to feed himself once a day, and you gave him everything we purchased for our big party. I am sure that, instead of delivering it at our home, he must have disappeared with everything. We must immediately go back to the market to find out more about the porter and then go to the police station to file a complaint against him."

  They both left towards the market. On their way, near the market, they saw another porter. They stopped him to inquire about the old porter but then noticed that he was carrying their stuff in his cart! The angry wife asked him, "Where is that old thief? This is our stuff and he was supposed to deliver it. It seems you thieves are stealing our stuff and are going to sell it".

  The porter replied, "Madam, please calm down. That poor old man was sick since last month. He wasn't even able to earn enough money to have one single meal a day. He was on his way to deliver your stuff, but he was hungry, sick, and couldn't gather the strength to go any further in this heat of the noon. He fell down and he handed me $15. His last words were: 'I have accepted an advance payment for this delivery, take this money and please deliver it to this address.'"

"Madam, He was hungry, he was poor, but he was an honest man. I was just on my way to complete the old man's last delivery at your home," the porter said. Upon hearing this, the husband had tears in his eyes, but his wife felt so ashamed, she did not even have the courage to look her husband in the eye.

Moral: Honesty has no class. Respect everyone regardless of their financial and social status. It's always a good deed to give something to the one who deserves.

永远不要杀害作者

[意大利] 苏珊·C.尼格拉

我的天哪！发生了什么事？以前从来没发生过这样的事。我陷入了困境，落入了陷阱，被困住了，走投无路，没有安全出口。以前总有突围脱险的办法，奇迹总是在最后一分钟出现，转危为安。

我回想了一下我是怎么到了这里的，我想起自己像往常一样被分配了案子。我去上班的时候，队长告诉我发生了一起谋杀案，他给我提供了案子的细节，然后我展开了调查。我没法告诉你，我怎么知道从哪里开始着手调查，但我就是知道。有时我从家庭成员入手，有时从工作地点入手，有时我也会从讯问死者的朋友入手。我一直都在寻找动机和凶杀第一现场，我会全身心地投入到这一切上面。

每宗案件都是独一无二、让人兴致盎然的，不过，这桩案子比我之前接手的都要迂回曲折。这桩案子的嫌疑人众多，每个人的作案动机各异，感觉就像有人在耍我。可能我是在做梦吧，等我醒来就会是新的一天，我就会接手新的案子，但是我每次着手新案子时，都是这种感觉。我就感觉自己在做白日梦，在重重迷雾中摸索调查。有时我也会幻想有一个木偶师在操纵我身上的细线，但是我从来没有把这些想法透露给别人，我不想让人听了觉得我有妄想症。

这段时间我都是独自一人，我亲爱的朋友兼搭档杰克在我们调查上一个案子时遇害了。到目前为止，我拒绝了所有的搭档请求。我依稀记得我和杰克是在大学里相识的，我们一起一步一步往上爬，甚至一起通过侦探考试，一起升职。我第一个案子之前的所有记忆都是模模糊糊的，就好像它从来没有发生过一样，只是在什么地方听过的故事。更奇怪的是，进入警察学院之前的事情我都不记得了。非常奇怪……我一直想问我是不是可能有某种心理创伤，这就是我不记得童年生活的原因，但我从来没有付诸行动。

杰克之前不仅仅是我的搭档，他还曾是我最好的朋友和爱人。我继承了他的遗志。我们能把对方没说完的话说完，通过奇特的、短暂的手语交流，这样的默契只有结婚多年的人才会有。我坚信如果杰克还在这里的话，我不会陷入这样的困境。我们总是肩并肩地作战。

我是瓦莱丽·多兹中尉。我是公认的、有史以来最出色的侦探之一。我对人有一种神奇的第六感，因而获得了出类拔萃的推理能力。每当我要结案的时候，我回忆案情，潜意识里已经知道了谁是凶手，调查只是搜集证据的例行程序而已。尽管我的名声由来已久，但我却被分区警察局的那些男人所忽略。他们都有一种病态的欲望，希望看到我出差错，所以他们总是充耳不闻。另外，我的队长喜欢我100%成功的破案率。我让他很有面子，他也心知肚明，这就是他总是把最棘手的案子交给我的原因，让我是个女人这个事实见鬼去吧。

而现在的我站在这里，恐惧万分，不知道该向哪个方向走，我盼望我还能有那种奇特的感觉，那种我有时感到时间闪回的感觉，闪回的时候，我所经历过的所有事都消失了，然后一切又重新开始了。我没有跟任何人说过这些，甚至对杰克都没有说，因为那样的话，我肯定他们会把我关进疯人院，把钥匙扔掉。他们说天才和疯子之间只有一条细细的线，可能我有的时候过界了，而我作为凶杀案警探，疯子的那一面正是我成功的关键所在。

我着手的每一桩案子里的所有事件，每一场谈话、每一次行动，全都是从我脑海中的叙述开始的。就好像我才自言自语了什么，接下来就立刻就发生了！你想知道还有比这更疯狂的吗……就是这样。当我叙述说我的嫌犯朝我打了一拳，我没有退缩，甚至都没闪躲。我只是脑子里想了一下嫌犯朝我挥拳，我没有退缩甚至都没有躲开。我只是叙述了一下我对此的反应，就像我用武术专长把嫌犯撂倒似的。你大概觉得这太疯狂了，但是我会在脑海里叙述每一个动作，就好像我是武术指导一样，嫌犯没有别的选择，只能按我期望的做。顺便说一下，我还总是赢呢！

去你的吧！我一直都没有打断脑海里的叙述，也拒绝深究。但是，该死的，现在它却告诉我在拐角处转弯，而就在这个拐角我会被枪杀。"去你的吧，我不会过去的！"现在我感觉有一双手推着我向那个方向走，但是我用高跟鞋死死地扎在地里，一英寸都不肯挪动。想想看，我从来没有像现在这样有自知之明，这么关注我脑海里的叙述。就好像雾气刚散，我第一次真正清醒。

推我后背的手越来越用力，我定在原地不肯向前。推的力量与我的意志之间的紧张局势一触即发，火星飞溅。火星导致空气中烟雾弥漫，就那时，我被托起来了，就在我被托起来时，"**砰**"的一声，爆炸了，我被气流顶到天上，掉到了一个陌生的房子里。

我环顾四周，看到一个老太太坐在电脑桌前工作。她目瞪口呆地看着我，好像惊讶于我的出现。我问："你是谁？我在哪里？"她回答道："我是作者。"这种解释根本没什么意义，所以我继续追问："请解释一下你说的话。"她回答说："你是我写的侦探小说的主角，可是我无论如何都不能理解你是怎样挣脱了命运,从我的书里悄无声息消失的。"

我这才恍然大悟,说:"这么说你就是我脑海里的那个声音……**你想要杀了我!为什么?**"

她说:"在我停止写这些愚蠢的侦探小说之前,我想把所有的关系都整理好,我讨厌书里的每一个人,但他们是我的面包和奶油,所以我不得不一直写下去,但是我现在靠你已经赚够了钱,我不想再写你了,再继续下去我会有很大的压力,所以我认为,如果我杀了你,那就一了百了了。"

我想着她说的话,越想越气。我下意识地慢慢举起持枪的右手,瞄准她扣动了扳机,说:**"去死吧,你这个忘恩负义的婊子!"**

后记

作者的邻居听到枪声,报了警。警察们赶到以后,发现书房里有两具尸体,一具伏在书桌上,另一具横在地板上。可以看出,桌子上的女人是遭到枪击而死的,但从外表看不出地板上女人的死因。

警探领队对他的搭档说:"这些'人物'什么时候才能学会不去杀死他们的作者呢?这对你来说是一个重要的教训,看在我们两人的分儿上,**请**不要杀我们的作者!"

Never Kill the Author

By Susan C. Nigra

Oh My God! What's happening? This has never happened before. I am cornered, trapped, boxed in with no safe way out. There has always been a way out before, miraculous last minute saves.

I think back to how I got here and I remember I was assigned this case as per usual. I show up for work and the Captain tells me there has been a murder, he gives me the details and then I begin my investigation. I can't tell you how I know where to start, I just do. Sometimes, I start with the family, sometimes the place of employment and sometimes I start by interviewing friends of the deceased; but all that is always after I examine the crime scene. I am constantly looking for motives, a place to start, something to sink my teeth into.

Every assignment is unique and interesting, but this one has had more convoluted twists and turns than any case I've had in the past. There are so many suspects, each with a different motive, making me feel like someone is playing a trick on me. Maybe I'm dreaming and I'll wake up to a new day and a new case, but that is the way I feel when I start each new case. I feel like I am daydreaming and walking through my investigation in a fog. I sometimes fantasize that there is a puppet master out there pulling my strings but I don't tell anyone, because I don't want to sound paranoid.

I'm alone this time since my dear friend and partner Jake, was killed while investigating our last case. I have vague memories of Jake and I starting out at the academy together and working our way up the ladder together, even passing the Detective's Exam and being promoted at the same time. All my memories before our first case are vague, almost as if it never happened, just memories of having heard the story somewhere. Even stranger is that I can't remember anything prior to entering the Police Academy. Very odd...I keep meaning to ask if I had some type of trauma and that's why I can't remember my childhood, but somehow I never get around to it.

Jake was more than my partner, he was my best friend and lover. I started where he left off. We finished each other's sentences and had that queer short hand communication that people who have been married a long time have. I have a strong conviction that if Jake were still here, I wouldn't be in this mess. We always watched each other's backs.

My name is Lt. Valerie Dodds and I am considered to be one of the most brilliant investigators that ever lived. I have extraordinary powers of deduction enhanced by an uncanny sixth sense about people. Once I close a case, I look back and realize that on a subliminal level, I already knew who did it, and the investigation is just the necessary steps to prove it. Even with a stellar reputation, I am still ignored by the men of my precinct. They have a pathological need for me to be wrong, so they choose not to listen. My Captain, on the other hand, likes my 100% success rate. I make him look good and he knows it, and that is why he assigns me the most difficult cases and to hell with the fact that I am a woman.

Right now, as I stand here terrified, not knowing which way to turn, I wish I would get that odd sensation that I get sometimes of moving backwards, and all the events are disappearing as I pass them, and then I start over. I don't speak to anyone about this, not even Jake; because for sure they'd lock me up in the loony bin and throw away the key. They say that there is a fine line between genius and insanity, so maybe I cross the line sometimes, and maybe that insanity is precisely the key to my success as a homicide detective.

All the events of each of my cases, every conversation, every activity all start as a narration in my head. It's like I say it to myself, and then it instantly is! You want to know what's even more insane...It's this; when I narrate my suspect throwing a punch at me, and I don't back away or even duck. And I just narrate my suspect throwing a punch at me, and I don't back away or even duck. I just narrate my reaction to it, like taking the suspect down with my expertise in martial arts. I know you will think this is nuts, but I narrate each move, as if I am choreographing the fight and the suspect doesn't have any choice but to respond as I expect him to. By the way, I always win!

HELL NO! Never before have I interrupted the narration in my head and refused to follow through. But damn, it's telling me to turn the corner where I'll be shot and killed. "Hell no, I won't go!" Now I feel hands shoving me in that direction but I dig my heels in and don't budge an inch. Come to think of it, never before have I been so self aware, so involved in my narrative. It's like the fog is lifting and I am waking up for the first time.

The hands on my back start to shove harder and harder and I hang on without moving forward. The tension between the shove and my will is explosive and sparks begin to fly. The sparks cause a smoky atmosphere in which I am lifted up and that's when it happens, BOOM, an explosion, and I am propelled into the air and land in a strange room.

I look around and I see an older woman sitting at her desk working on her computer. She is looking at me, mouth agape, as if she is shocked by my arrival. "Who are you and where am I?" I ask. She says, "I am the Author." This means nothing to me, so I continue: "Please explain yourself." She replies, "You are the main character in the detective novels that I write, and for the life of me, I can't figure out how you resisted your destiny and popped out of my book."

Then it dawns on me and I say, "So you're the voice in my head...YOU TRIED TO KILL ME! Why?"

"I wanted to tie up all loose ends before I stop writing these stupid detective novels," she said. "I've hated each and every one of them, but they were my bread and butter, so I had to, but now you have made me enough money that I don't have to write you anymore. I was getting a lot of pressure to continue, so I figured, if I killed you off; that would be the end of it once and for all."

I thought about what she said and I began to become more and more angry. I didn't even realize I was slowly raising my right arm with the gun still in hand, and pointing it at her and as I pulled the trigger, I said : "DIE, YOU UNGRATEFUL BITCH."

Epilogue

The Author's neighbor heard the gun shot and called the police. When they arrived and found the study, they saw two bodies, one dead at her desk and the other dead on the floor. The woman at the desk had been shot, but there was no outward sign of the cause of death of the other woman that was lying on the floor.

The lead detective turned to his partner and said, "When are these 'characters' going to learn not to kill their Authors? This is an important lesson for you, for both our sakes, PLEASE, never ever kill our Author!"

译 后 记

常常有初涉翻译的同学问我,做好翻译需要哪些过程?其实,这跟做其他学术研究也没有什么不同,无非还是那"三板斧"——理论、历史、实践。具体到翻译上,就是翻译理论,包括具有描述、解释、预测功能的纯翻译理论,以及指导功能的应用翻译理论,具有借鉴功能的翻译史,还具有实用功能的翻译实践。

法国哲学家帕斯卡说过:"智慧胜于知识。"如果说,知识回答的"是什么",那么,智慧回答的就是"怎么样"和"为什么"。对于翻译来说,翻译理论和翻译史解决的是宏观层面"何为译"的问题;文化,特别是语言对比解决的是"译何为"的问题;从语法、逻辑、修辞三个维度审视翻译实践解决"如何译"的问题。当然,翻译是一个需要 know something about everything 的专业,也就是 "you don't need to know everything about something, but you need to know a little bit of everything",掌握一些翻译辅助工具也很有必要。

对于翻译理论,我曾在专著《翻译基础指津》(中译出版社,2017年)中有过专题阐述,这里就不再赘述,说到底,科学的核心是理论,没有理论,你的研究将一无所有。

对于翻译理论与实践之间的关系，要明确的是离开实践的理论是空洞的理论，离开理论的实践是盲目的实践。

翻译是一种看似门槛很低、实则难度很高的学术。其实，不是学语言的都是学英语的；不是学英语的都能做翻译；不是做翻译的什么文体都能翻译。相对于母语创作来说，翻译创作的难度更高。对于英语专业来说，听说读写译，最难莫过于翻译；对于各种翻译文体来说，最难莫过于文学翻译。至于翻译标准，我觉得上下文，也只有上下文，才是决定词义、段义、句义、文义的唯一标准。这个上下文可以是上一个词和下一个词，也可以是上一句和下一句，或者是上一段和下一段，甚至是上一章和下一章，乃至同一作者所著的上一部作品和下一部作品。具体践行到中观层面，双语差异之处，便是困难之时。到了微观层面，译得通不通是语法问题，译得对不对是逻辑问题，译得好不好是修辞问题。

下面，就以之前翻译的图书为例，来做一简要的实证。

一、逻辑

例 1. Do you understand what condoms are used for?

你知道安全套是用来做什么的吗？

——《谋杀的颜色》

（原文中被问的是一个 14 岁的孩子，所以 condom 虽然是一个专有名词，通常选择一个义项即可，但考虑到孩子对性的有限认知,这里只能译成"安全套",不能译成"避孕套"。)

例2. She had been older than he then in Ohio. Now she was not young at all. Bill was still young.

当年在俄亥俄州的时候她就比他大,现在,她毕竟已经不再年轻,而比尔却不见老。

——译趣坊第一辑《时光不会辜负有爱的人》之《初秋》

(原文 Bill was still young 是肯定形式,译文转换成了否定形式,但内容没有变,反而更为准确。)

例3. God made Coke, God made Pepsi, God made me, oh so sexy, God made rivers, God made lakes, God made you...well we all make mistakes.

上帝创造了可口可乐,上帝创造了百事可乐,上帝创造了我,哦,多么性感。上帝创造了河流,上帝创造了湖泊,上帝创造了你……怎么说呢,谁能不出错呢?

——译趣坊第一辑《人生是一场意外的遇见》之《毒舌段子》

(原文的 well we all make mistakes 译成了"怎么说呢,谁能不出错呢?"肯定变否定,句号变问号,但内在的逻辑始终如一。)

二、语法

例1. "Do you think all these people are happy with the wonderful things they have?" She asked.

"People happy with things? No, no," the old man said. "Only people make people happy. You just have to know how to love people. People aren't things; people think, they feel. You have to tell them you love them. You have to show them. You have to say nice things. You have to mean them…"

"你觉得这些拥有好东西的人幸福吗?"她问道。

"拥有东西的人幸福?不对,不对,"老人说道,"只有人才能让人幸福。你需要知道怎么去爱别人就够了。人不是东西;人会思考,人有感觉。你要告诉别人你爱他们,你要把爱展示给他们看。你要说金玉良言,要有真情实感……"

——译趣坊第一辑《愿你出走半生 归来仍是少年》之《幸福在哪里》

(关于一词多义,就是要"确认过眼神,选择对的含义"。原文的 wonderful things 在上下文中有哲学意味,指代的是物质,这里在讨论的实际上是物质和精神与幸福之间的关系,所以译成"东西";You have to say nice things 里的 things 指的是话语,所以译成了"金玉良言"。)

例 2. Saying goodbye in autumn is not saying goodbye forever.

对秋天说再见,秋天还会见。

——《英汉经典阅读系列散文卷》之《乡村之秋》

(关于句法翻译,要分析原文的句子成分,先找出主谓宾,然后找出定状补,确定句意。双语能"神同步"真真是极好的。不能就或分或合,或缩或扩,或换序,或变性、变态,甚至十八般武艺并用,舍"形"而取"义"。从语言层次的转换情况来看,既可以是同一层次的同类型转换,也可以是同一层次的非同类型转换,还可以是超越同一层次的转换。从本句来看,译文做了分句处理,属于同一类型的非同类型转换。)

例3. I loved you enough to accept you for what you are, not what I wanted you to be.

我爱你至深,才接受你现在的样子,尽管不是我期望的样子。

——译趣坊第一辑《时光不会辜负有爱的人》之《爱你至深》

(关于从句翻译,原文的 what you are 和 what I wanted you to be 实现了从句译成词组,句型由抽象向具体的转换。)

例4. They are hard to find when your eyes are closed, but they are everywhere you look when you choose to see.

选择合上双眼,天使很难发现;选择睁大双眼,天使会在任何地方出现。

——译趣坊第二辑《生命中一直在等待的那一天》之《天使何所似》

(英文重形合,句子成分"一个都不能少",所以连词、关系词、介词多,译成汉语,很多时候,一省了之。原文的 when 和 but 就是如此。)

例5. "You're a very good dancer," she sighed.

"你的舞跳得好好啊!"她叹道。

——译趣坊第三辑《愿我们每个人都被世界温柔以待》之《下雨天,留人天》

(在翻译过程中,英汉两种语言的词类或词性均会经常发生转换。没有什么词是不能"变性"的,本句原文的名词 dancer 就译成了动词"跳"。从本质上讲,汉语是一种多运用动词的语言,是真正的"动感地带"。)

三、修辞

例1. Alarmed, sad? He smiled, and his smile kept on getting broader, and before long, he was dissolving into laughter. He was determined to control himself, but this resistance collapsed completely. He started guffawing loudly…

感到奇怪?难过?他微微笑着,接着,嘴越咧越大,迸发出一声大笑,他想自控,但这一抵抗立刻土崩瓦解了,竟哈哈大笑不止。

——译趣坊第一辑《愿你出走半生 归来仍是少年》之《幸福的人》

(这是层递修辞格,程度递增,直译过来,一目了然。)

例2. May you always walk your path with love. May you always help your fellow travelers along the way. And may your roads always lead you Home again.

愿你的人生之路都有爱为伴,愿你在旅途中帮助同路人,愿你人生中的一段又一段旅程都是通往回"家"的路。

——译趣坊第二辑《所有的路 最终都是回家的路》之《所有的路,最终都是回家的路》

(这是重复修辞格,译文三个"愿你",一一对应,句句对应,原文 roads 的复数得到强化翻译,作为全篇收尾的画龙点睛之笔。)

例3. Even more than what they eat I like their intellectual grasp. It is wonderful. Just watch them read. They simply read all the time.

我喜欢他们的饮食,但是我更喜欢他们学富五车。那真是了不起。看看他们看的书就一目了然了。他们简直就是手不释卷。

——译趣坊第三辑《如果事与愿违 请相信一定另有安排》之《怎样成为百万富翁》

(修辞翻译也可以"无中生有",本句中的 intellectual grasp 译成"学富五车"、read all the time 译成"手不释卷",也都毫无违和感。)

例4. Neither manifested the least disposition to retreat. It was evident that their battle-cry was "Conquer or die".

双方都没有一丝一毫的退却表现,显然他们的战争口号是"不成功便成仁"。

——译趣坊第三辑《选一种姿态 让自己活得无可替代》之

《红蚂蚁大战黑蚂蚁》

（修辞可以让你的译文变得更有腔调。"想要有腔调，就不能说大白话，得加上装饰"。原文中的 Conquer or die 是一个仿拟修辞格，以归化的策略套译成"不成功便成仁"，来描绘双方死战的状态，成为亲切的"中国风"。）

Language is shaped by, and shapes, human thought. 这句话的意思是"人的思想形成语言，而语言又影响了人的思想。"文学翻译是一个在各美其美、美人之美的基础上，力争美美与共的过程。原作者的思想形成了原作者的语言，原作者的语言又影响了我的思想。文学翻译让我意识到：文学的终极使命，是一种灵魂的救赎，我庆幸自己此生在一个不合时宜的时空做了一件不合时宜的事情，它唤醒了我心中一个蠢蠢欲动的自己。我爱这个自己，我相信文学"他者"的魔力，可以让一只匍匐的虫豸，陡然生出纵横天地的心，化茧成蝶。

让"译趣坊系列"也带你飞。

张白桦
2020 年大暑于塞外古城

图书在版编目（CIP）数据

与自己和解　才能与世界温柔相处：英汉对照/（加）斯蒂芬·里柯克等著；张白桦译.—北京：中国国际广播出版社，2021.5
（译趣坊.世界微型小说精选）
ISBN 978-7-5078-4887-8

Ⅰ.①与… Ⅱ.①斯…②张… Ⅲ.①小小说－小说集－世界－现代－汉、英 Ⅳ.①I14

中国版本图书馆CIP数据核字（2021）第064474号

与自己和解　才能与世界温柔相处（中英双语）

著　　者	［加拿大］斯蒂芬·里柯克 等
译　　者	张白桦
策　　划	张娟平
责任编辑	笑学婧
校　　对	张　娜
设　　计	国广设计室
出版发行	中国国际广播出版社［010-83139469　010-83139489（传真）］
社　　址	北京市西城区天宁寺前街2号北院A座一层 邮编：100055
印　　刷	环球东方（北京）印务有限公司
开　　本	880×1230　1/32
字　　数	145千字
印　　张	7.75
版　　次	2021年6月 北京第一版
印　　次	2021年6月 第一次印刷
定　　价	35.00元

版权所有　盗版必究